THE LUST LIST: MILES RIOT

HEART STRINGS

MIRA BAILEE

NoMi Press

Euphoria Publishing
NoMi Press
www.euphoriapublishing.com

Publisher's Note: This is a work of fiction. Names, characters, places,
and incidents are a product of the author's imagination, and any
resemblance to actual people, living or dead, or to businesses, com-
panies, events, institutions, or locales is completely coincidental.

ISBN-13: **978-0692618844**
ISBN-10: **0692618848**

Printed in the United States of America

Dedicated to everyone

who's leaped out of their comfort zone

and found an adventure on the other side.

Chapter One

Abby

I swear I'm trying. I'm willing to keep an open mind. I can almost make myself believe this is my scene. But just a minute ago a crowd surfer almost kicked me in the face—a shirtless, sweaty, hairy man holding a bottle of cheap beer. His scuffed up, stained shoe was close enough, I could smell it. Or maybe that was just the scent of pot smoke and body odor mixing in the closed space.

So I'm still trying, but for now, I'm staking my claim on a bar stool in the back. There's almost enough oxygen at this end of the bar to breathe in a full toxic breath. Cigarette smoke, liquor, and the musty smell of three hundred bodies smashed together in front of a stage assault my senses, along with the amps threatening to blow holes through my ear drums and the foggy haze that obstructs my view of the stage.

Vitriol is playing their last show in the swampy hole-in-the-wall, Dazed. It's more than evident they've outgrown the place. For the past few weeks, they've expanded to amphitheaters and concert halls, but they call this place home. It's where they got their start, and they wanted a farewell show with their most loyal fans before tomorrow, when they hit the road on their first, large-scale cross-country tour.

I'm not sure which the fans love more—the chaotic energy of angry rock music or the seductive nature of the lead singer, Kennedy Rose. Her platinum hair cascades to her thighs, longer than the skin-tight leather shorts she's wearing over fishnets. Her skin is porcelain and decked out in tattoos and several layers of carefully applied makeup. We all can't help but be drawn to her crimson-stained lips as she belts out the bridge of their song, "Tempted by Fate". The crowd sings along.

To her left, a bass player head bangs—his stick-straight mohawk moving along with him without a hair falling out of place. His fingers move faster than any bass player I've seen before and after he finishes a solo, he looks back to the audience and beams a mischievous grin. The women in the crowd scream.

In the back, the drummer seems to be in his own world. Maybe he's caught up in the moment. Maybe he's on drugs. Who knows?

But he never misses a beat. "Tempted by Fate" comes to an end, but he doesn't stop playing, transitioning to the next song seamlessly. The energy of the bar intensifies, not a second to catch your breath in between one loud song and another. It's exhausting, yet the crowd dances on.

The guitarist sticks to the shadows for the most part—the outlier in this quartet since the rest of them seem to be fighting for the spotlight. His disheveled hair covers half his face, and the bar lights glint of a lip ring. His torn jeans reveal tattoos on his legs, and I'll assume there's just as much ink on the rest of his body, though the long sleeve shirt he's wearing—Is he insane? It's a thousand degrees in here—keep that a mystery. As the verse of "Clementine Concubine" transitions to the chorus, he steps forward to his own mic, offering backing vocals. He growls and croons as Kennedy covers a vocal range that even I can find impressive. The instruments get lower and lower as the two sing, their voices taking over everyone's senses. Then a brief pause of silence before everything picks back up, louder and faster than before. The crowd seems mesmerized.

It's no wonder Vitriol is on the cusp of being signed by a major label. If they can grow a fan base as committed as these sweaty, thrashing twenty-somethings, then they can—

"How—out—ere?" The voice suddenly at my left ear almost makes me jump out of my skin. The volume level has been raised to 'impossible' and I didn't see this guy coming. A tall man with dreadlocks and jeans that have been ripped into shorts lingers over me.

"What?" I yell.

"I—you want—ere?"

I have no idea what he's saying. Is this one of those smile and nod situations, pretend like I understood him the second time? Isn't there some sort of unspoken rule—only ask someone to repeat what they said once? After that, it's far too awkward to ask again. You might as well act like you heard him just fine. But my eyes—squinting with confusion—give me away.

"Beer!" he shouts even louder. "You want one?"

Comprehension washes over me. At first, I could've sworn he was asking me to get out of here—with him—a total stranger. Creepy.

"No thanks," I shout. My voice will be gone tomorrow if this guy tries to strike up a conversation.

The song ends and Vitriol leaves the stage. The crowd begins chanting, "Encore, encore!"

"My treat," this guy next to me says. "You look lonely."

"I'm not." I turn back toward the stage waiting for the inevitable reappearance of the band and the final song.

"You aren't one of those straight-edge chicks, are you?"

"And what if I am?" I'm not, but who's he to judge?

The guy laughs, throwing his head back like he's never heard of anything more ridiculous. "Then you're in the wrong place. There's enough secondhand smoke to get you lung cancer *and* a contact high."

Quite the charmer, this one. "Good thing I'm about to leave then."

"You like the show?"

You'd think I would've struck out with my other answers. "It was all right." I'm not about to admit this was my first, and hopefully last time watching Vitriol and anything like Vitriol. Definitely not my taste in music.

"There's another show down the street later. This band, Kickoff. Wanna go with me?"

"Are you asking me out?" Now it's my turn to laugh. "You haven't even asked me my name, but it doesn't matter. It's a 'no' anyway. No *thanks*." Can't forget my manners.

"Man, you must be one of those tight ass chicks. Gotta loosen up. You can come to my car and smoke a joint with me."

He's beginning to entertain me more than the concert did. "But aren't I one of those straight-edge *chicks*?"

"It's good to try new things." He reaches up and brushes a sweaty hand over my cheek. Too far, buddy.

I pull away, trying to hide the disgust from my face. "I said no to your offers already. I'm not interested."

He mutters something—"Bitch", I'm pretty sure. But the volume has been turned back up to 'catastrophically deafening' as the guitarist of Vitriol runs back on stage. The rest of the band remains unseen.

"Last chance, babe," Mr. Dreadlocks says. "You came here for fun. I'll make sure you have some."

The guitarist begins to play. *Miles. Miles Riot*—that's his name, I remember.

"I didn't come for fun," I correct the relentless ass. "I came for work."

But Miles starts playing, and it's, thankfully, too loud for any more conversation.

"What?" the guy shouts.

I look back at him one more time and yell as loud as I can. "I'm here for my job."

The same look of confusion I possessed earlier takes over his face. He still can't hear me. I take my phone from my pocket and open a text application, typing in "NOT INTER-ESTED!"

I flash the screen toward him and wave a goodbye, moving into the crowd to disappear. The song is surprisingly slower than all the others, so it's easier to weave through all the bodies. When I'm certain I'm concealed enough to not have Dreads track me down again, I pocket my phone, and count down the minutes to the end of this show. Almost done.

Miles is bathed in a single spotlight and the crowd sings along with every word—proving I'm probably the only one who doesn't know this song.

"*And to you...I say...adieu...*" they all sing as one big choir.

My personal bubble is being smashed on all sides as people move closer and closer to the stage. Can't they see just fine where they are?

Then the spotlight goes off. The stage goes pitch black.

The music stops.

In the next seconds, too much happens too fast to comprehend. The crowd shifts forward. My back is shoved. The lights come on all at once. And the music kicks back on full gear—all four members on the stage again.

Another shove, this time from my right side. I'm ready to get defensive when I'm pushed from the opposite side. The floor of bodies is moving in waves—side-to-side, backward-and-forward. A hole opens up around me, and I don't know where to go. Kennedy sings. Miles strums. The song grows with more energy by the second. And I find myself in the middle of a mosh pit.

Groups of people take turns pushing and shoving, ramming their bodies into surrounding people who slam back into them. I'm hit from the front by a girl in combat boots. I'm shoved in the back by someone smaller, yet much stronger than I am. I try to push through the circle to escape, but they take the wrong cue and excitedly push me back into the flailing moshers.

"Get me out of this!" I scream at the top of my lungs to a buff guy in a white tank top.

Again, he takes the wrong cue as he lifts me up effortlessly. Other arms reach up to support my body over their heads. Now I'm above the crowd, staring at the ceiling as countless hands trade off carrying me. I can only think back to the crowd surfer that almost kicked me in the face. Now, I'm focused solely on my own feet, grateful I skipped the heels tonight. *Please don't let me hurt anyone.*

Oh wait, *please don't let* me *get hurt!*

The stage is getting closer and closer, and if I'm not already terrified, horror rushes through me. I do *not* want to be dumped off on the stage for all to see.

"Turn, turn, turn," I plead, as if anyone can hear me. But the stage draws nearer. *Oh no.*

I catch the edge of the crowd and realize I have no idea how to get down. I'm just going to plummet to the ground and scurry away. I started this night *trying* to immerse myself. Trying to be okay with what may be eating up the next week of my life. But seven feet off the ground, floating horizontally, trusting the hands of drunk concertgoers...I'm done trying.

Suddenly another face emerges beyond the backs of a bunch of sweaty heads. Two huge arms reach for me, waiting.

A bouncer is coming to my rescue.

As quickly—albeit awkwardly—as he gets me to the ground, I hurry out of the bar. I've seen enough. I've *experienced* enough. I'm done. And not just with this evening.

The cool night breeze hits me as I push through the doors, and I suck in a deep breath of clean air and close my eyes for a second. No way in hell can I do this again.

I reach for my phone as I start walking away. The last song ends, and I round the corner of the building just as the front doors swing open—ecstatic fans pouring into the empty street. It's quieter back here as I dial my boss's number. After a couple rings, I hear Jonathan pick up.

"Abby. You have any idea what time it is?"

"Trust me, I do." No need to be rude. I inhale trying to calm my nerves. Adrenaline is rushing through me—my hands and legs are still shaky from my near-death experience. Okay, that's dramatic, but still. That was some scary stuff. How can people enjoy it? "Sorry," I tell Jonathan. "I just needed to call and tell you I can't do the assignment. I'm sure there are plenty of others who'd jump at the chance, so can we just switch some things around and—"

"You woke me up to tell me you're quitting?"

"No-no-no. I just can't do the assignment. I'll take any other, just not this one. I'll even do that one story—you know, the one about the pageant girl who's now doing that mix of yodeling and harmonica?"

"Yeah, sounds to me like you don't want your job anymore." Jonathan's tone is light, but I know what he's trying to do.

"I definitely *do* want my job. I love working for Lydian Magazine. But—"

"Great. I'm glad you're taking the assignment then. Enjoy the scenery!"

He hangs up before I can argue any further. Believe it or not, Jon and I are friends. But the boss side of him takes no nonsense, and that clearly includes music journalists trying to turn down music journalism assignments. He also has this thing with pushing me out of my comfort zone—as if that's not obvious here.

So it's all or nothing. Apparently, I'm going on tour with Vitriol.

A nearby back door opens and roadies carry out amps and instrument cases. Another one walks out with a rolled up rug over his shoulder and a set list in his hand. They head to a smaller trailer attached to a pickup truck parked behind a bus. Right after they disappear back inside, the band members begin their exit.

First, the bassist. I think his name is Nate. He carries his own guitar case, and his free arm is draped around the half-naked hips of a tall brunette. She's smoking and holds her hand up to let Nate take a puff. I catch enough scent to know it's definitely not a cigarette.

Next, a female voice from inside threatens, "You better fucking not." As she emerges, I see Kennedy with a phone to her ear. "No. We agreed on tonight... Yeah. I'm still coming." She lowers her voice to a seductive tone. "And so will you."

Nate and the woman clinging to him go inside the bus. Kennedy stops short and calls to him. "Nate, you know the rules. If you're gonna screw her, make it quick. We need to get out of here."

I feel my own cheeks flush at the candidness as the girl with Nate giggles and says to him, "Well, you heard her."

"Oh, for fuck's sake." Kennedy's got a mouth on her. My mama would not be proud. I turn to see who she's yelling at now. Two men are walking this way, camera's pressed to their faces as they take a steady stream of shots.

While journalists are the busy bees of entertaining news stories, paparazzi—or papa-*ratzzi*, as I see it—are the disease-ridden rodents infesting everyone's homes and livelihoods. Of course, a lot of people bulk us together, and I've received my fair share of hostility. But I need to talk to someone in Vitriol. I need to introduce myself and prepare for tomorrow when I'll be cramped on that bus with them. These guys, now practically in Kennedy's face, are going to make this extra hard for me to find my opening and break the ice.

Kennedy's off the phone now, pointing an angry finger at one of the ratz. "Don't you have more important people to violate? Get out of here, you pieces of shit!" Just then, the back door to Dazed opens again. Kennedy swings around and sees it's her drummer. "Dax, deal with these assholes."

Still looking as dazed as he did on stage, I'm not sure how Kennedy expects him to get rid of them. She's probably the most vocal of them all. What's Dax going to do? Stare them down with his intensely dark eyes?

He waltzes up to the first rat, the one closest to Kennedy, and shoves his hand into his camera. The camera, being near his face, slams into the guy's right eye, and there's a crunch where the side of the camera's body hits his nose hard. He falls to the ground, the camera hitting the pavement, and I watch as a small trickle of blood streams out of his nostrils.

Holy crap.

Just as quickly as Dax drops the first one, he moves to the second, swinging a fist that connects with the guy's mouth. This one tries to fight back, letting his camera dangle on its strap around his neck and shoving Dax with both arms. Dax grabs him by the elbows and shoves a knee into his groin. The rat—well, now I feel bad thinking of him like that, they're getting brutalized. The pap hunches over trying to brace himself, not giving up on the fight.

Eyes wide, I can only stand and watch. What should I do? I could call the cops and make instant enemies with Vitriol. I could say something and try to stop it, but I doubt a random stranger will have much effect on them. Others have found their way over to this side of the building too. Scantily-dressed women and a lot of guys wearing all black. Some of them snap photos with their phones while others cheer Dax on. This is preposterous. I should step in and say something...

Miles comes out of the bar, unsuspecting. The fight catches him by surprise, but I don't think I need to get involved anymore. "Hey!" He runs to Dax and pulls him away. "What the hell, man?" He surveys the scene. One guy on the ground. Another bent over in pain. An expensive camera tossed on the sidewalk. Kennedy and Dax still reeling with anger and aggression. "Paps?" he asks Kennedy.

She nods. "Have no sense of people's privacy." She looks down at the two cameramen. "And I don't feel bad for kicking your asses."

I almost laugh as she takes credit for Dax's work. Miles shakes his head disapprovingly. "Great start, guys. Let's not do this at every stop on the tour, 'kay?"

The paparazzi help each other to standing and hobble away. "You get a decent shot?" I hear one ask.

"Damn right," the other answers. "And it's gonna make the front page."

Unbelievable. After all that, and they're just happy they got the story they wanted. See what I mean? Ratz.

Kennedy and Dax disappear onto the bus with Miles behind them. A second later, the girl who'd gone in there with Nate comes back out, adjusting her barely-there skirt and looking deeply satisfied. A woman behind me takes notice, and tells her friend, "She got to bang one of them. I'm going to too, dammit. I'm way hotter." Her friend giggles, and my stomach turns.

The bus door still stands open, and before these other girls rush to it, I need to finish what I came here to do. I start forward, my pulse pounding in my ears. Impulsive, violent, reckless. How am I supposed to fit in with this band? This is insane.

I stop a couple feet short of the bus door. *Thanks a lot, Jonathan.* This is the opposite of the perfect job for me.

Suck it up, buttercup. At the end of the day, I'm still a professional. I can do this.

Now I just need to walk onto this bus.

In three...two...one.

* * *

Miles

"It's our last night in L.A., and you're getting into fights with fucking media?" The night had been a success up to this point. Great show. Great energy. A farewell to those who got us here. Tomorrow we leave California, starting a four-week national tour, playing at venues bigger than we'd ever imagined. This is a great fucking moment for Vitriol. Leave it to my jackass bandmates to try and screw it up. Kennedy's locked herself in the one bedroom in the back of the bus, and I'm waiting for an explanation from Dax or Nate.

"Don't stick up for them." Dax stands up like he's going to confront me. He knows not to lay a finger on me. "Your sister needed help. Where were you?"

"Inside talking to Eddie. You know? The guy who's bent over backward to help make all this happen? He's going to rip you a new asshole when he sees the tabloids tomorrow."

Nate looks amused, slouched in the corner of a couch. I stare down my bassist. "And what the hell were you doing?"

"A five-foot-seven beauty who likes to be on top," he answers with no hesitation.

I shake my head. Sex is Nate's way of finishing every show. It's like a ritual to him at this point.

Dax laughs and high fives Nate, plopping down next to him and turning back to me. "If you really cared, you'd run inside right now and tattle on us like a fucking five year old. Get out there and find yourself a bang. You need to relax."

They're like brothers I never wanted. We spend more time arguing and harassing each other than anything else. But they do give good advice. I need to get laid.

Outside, a sea of people wait to see if we'll hang out with them or fuck them. I see enough exposed belly buttons and lip gloss to know I have a magnificent share of options tonight.

I step outside and see a short blond first. She seems timid and scared but is the closest one to the bus. Good for her, building up that courage. She's cute, but not my type at all. I'm into confident women, those who know what they like, what they want, and go after it.

"Hi, Miles," the blond girl says, clearing her throat. "Real quick, I just wanted to—"

"You're sweet," I tell her, giving her my trademark grin. "I'm a little busy though, all right? I bet there's a nice guy in the crowd for you."

I keep walking, my eyes settling on two women who are nearly identical twins. They both have long wavy hair—one dyed deep red and the other, light blue—like fire and ice, and the seductive gaze I'm getting from both pairs of emerald eyes is promising. But I'm not into family affairs, if you know what I mean. "Sisters?" I ask them.

"Best friends," one answers.

"Perfect."

I'll take them back to my place on the beach where my king sized bed and a bottle of tequila await. The three of us walk back to the bus—groans of disappointment sounding off behind us. I won't lie. I get off on how much these ladies want to get on me. Nothing better than an ego boost accompanying un-limited opportunities for orgasms. The two ladies flanking me have no idea what they're in for tonight. I love pleasing them just as much as they love pleasing me, and tonight, it's double the pleasure.

As we near the bus, I see Eddie sprint out of Dazed. "Miles, hold up a second."

Damn. I'm ready to play, but my work isn't done.

"Why don't you ladies go inside, but stay away from the others. I don't share women with them." I give them each a kiss on their soft, wet lips. "Touch them, and I won't touch you," I say in a lower growl.

One of them squeals while the other sighs, and they both step up onto the bus. I remind myself to get their names at some point.

"Whatcha need, Ed?" I try not to sound annoyed. Our manager has done a lot to get us off the ground fast. Not only did he coordinate this tour, he hooked us up with a top-of-the line tour bus—luxury shit—and he's got several big name labels watching us closely. That's the main reason I can't have the rest of the band screwing things up.

Eddie stops next to the short, blond girl, still standing where I left her. Can she not take a hint? But then Eddie looks at her, looks at me, and says, "I need you to meet Abigail Clarke."

"Abby," she corrects him.

"Abby," Eddie repeats. "This is Miles."

"I know," she says, smiling. "It's nice to meet you."

Great. He's trying to hook me up with a groupie. Must be his cousin or something. I don't do those kinds of favors though, and fire and ice are inside ready to shake up all the earth's elements.

"Abby is a journalist with Lydian Magazine. She'll be writing a feature on Vitriol, and to do so, she'll be joining you for the first week of your tour."

Hold everything. Did he just say what I think he said?! A journalist is going on tour with us? It's hard enough keeping media away, and Eddie's invited one right onto our bus? He's out of his fucking mind. "Sounds great." I put an arm around Eddie. "Mind if we talk for a second?"

We get on the bus, and I close the door behind us. "Five minutes ago, I broke up a fight between Dax and the paparazzi. We *cannot* have one of them on this bus."

"She's not pap. She's legit. And she's helping get you all visible—in a positive light."

I notice we have an audience of curious eyes. Nate, Dax, and Kennedy lounge on one couch taking shots of whiskey and tequila. My fire and ice pseudo-twins stand on the other side. They're all looking our way, waiting to be filled in.

"Eddie's invited the tabloids to tour with us," I say bluntly. The easiest way to prove this is a bad idea is to let the rest of the band react to the announcement.

"The fuck?"

"You're joking."

"No way in hell."

They're a predictable chorus and give me just the response I needed.

I turn back to Eddie. "You know how much time I spend doing damage control around here? When we're out there," I nod toward the windows and the public world beyond, "I work full-time trying to keep the drama under wraps. I break up the fights, I keep the assholes away from Kennedy. I solve all the fucking problems. But when I'm in here, I'm not doing it. This is our privacy you're invading by letting that woman in. She's going to learn things she shouldn't, and that's all going to hit the pages of a magazine for the public to read. You *know* why that's a bad idea. You think any label will take us then? Did you think about that? How's that beneficial to any of us? It's not an option. She has to leave."

Eddie lets me get out my rant. He wanders to the table of shot glasses and fills two of them with the nearly empty bottle of whiskey. He hands me one. "You're the king, Miles. I get that. But when it comes to your career, I'm your god. I'm calling the shots here, and Abby stays. Drink up." He clinks his glass with mine and downs the shot before opening the bus door and leaving. As he passes Abby, he pats her on the shoulder and tells her to come in here.

I watch as the hesitant woman takes a deep breath and joins us on the bus. This is not going to go well.

I drink my shot, toss the empty glass to Nate, and stomp off the bus. Screw this. I'm not here to make friends with the person who can tear us down.

Leave it to Nate, though. I'm not two feet away from the bus when I hear him say, "At least she's hot."

Chapter Two

Abby

Last night did not go well. "It was a mess, Chord." Yes, I'm talking to my golden retriever. The tour bus leaves soon, and my bag's nearly packed. "The music is too much. The chaos is too much. The attitudes of the band members...too much. I'll be lucky to survive the first day."

Chord wanders out toward the kitchen and loudly slurps from his water bowl. Go figure, he's a terrible listener. I return to packing, but laugh. What do you take on a cross-country rock tour? My usual—jeans, cowboy boots, cute blazers—they're far too small town Texas girl for this, which is precisely why Jonathan should've known better than to send me on this assignment. It feels like one big practical joke. I sort through my belongings and settle on tank tops and a few spring dresses. The boots can stay home, but I'm not leaving behind my sandals and heels. Add my curling iron and some wide headbands, and I should last a week without looking too out of place.

I look around my studio. It's a small space, simple and homey. Leather couches sit in front of my TV with a thick, cream rug on the floor to designate my 'living room'. I'm on the opposite side next to my platform bed— unmade and loaded with extra pillows. My wardrobe holds all my necessities, including the framed photos sitting on top—my mom and I after I graduated from the University of

Texas, my sister with her newborn [son], and an older family photo from when I was thirteen, the last one taken before my dad passed away. I'm a long way from home, both in distance and lifestyle. I never expected Los Angeles would be a city where I'd settle, but after finishing school at UT Austin, my dream job at Unwired Press in Dallas hadn't opened up yet, and Lydian was too good an opportunity to pass up. Of course, it's assignments like this—following a wild rock band on tour—that makes me want to kick myself for ever taking this job to begin with. I could be back home, sitting on the front porch, listening to nature instead of highways, eating home-cooked meals instead of fast food.

I'll go back home someday.

My doorbell rings, interrupting my daydreaming. "Chord, that's for you, buddy."

I go to the door and let in Dee, my friend and coworker who's offered to pet sit while I'm gone. She opens her arms wide for a hug, her smooth, dark skin is hot from the midday sun. "You must be so excited. I'm jealous."

I laugh. "Something like that."

She comes in and makes herself at home. I love that about her. Must be because she grew up in Georgia. We both understand the need for hospitality and comfort, so when we hang out, we're either taking care of each other or acting like we've lived together our whole lives. Dee drops into my armchair, patting the side to invite Chord over. "We're going to have such a good week, aren't we sweetie?" Chord smothers her in kisses. Dee looks up at me. "You have everything ready?"

"I don't think I could ever be ready for this." Her comforting laugh makes me worry less. "Let me get you a drink. Water? Sweet tea?"

"Water's fine. And it'll be a great experience for you. So what if it's not your dream gig. You're branching out. You never know, you might even become a fan by the end of things."

I laugh. I get her a drink, dropping a couple slices of lemon into the water and bring it over. "My plan right now is to find the quickest story possible, draft it, and go home. If I'm lucky, I can be back here in a couple days."

Dee shakes her head and pulls her ponytail loose, letting her black curls fall. "Live for the moment, girl." She shakes her hand through her hair and sinks down further into the seat, relaxing. "You never know when unexpected things will happen. Like your band, Vitriol. I bet that guy from it wasn't expecting to see *ScandalLust* this morning."

Back to the tabloid talk. We're both college-educated journalists, we both take our jobs seriously, yet our topics of conversation always lead back to the trashy mags. I promised myself I'd never stoop to tabloid level, but I'll admit, it's a little fun seeing the crap they come up with.

"Was it about the fight last night?"

"What fight?" She sits up straighter, intrigued.

I fill her in on Dax beating up the pap ratz.

When I finish, her eyes get wider. "See what I mean? You'd never have been there to witness it if you kept to your old ways, staying in your comfortable little box."

"I like my comfortable little box, thank you very much. Now what were you talking about? What other trouble did they get in last night?"

She reaches into her purse and pulls out her tablet. This is the device she writes stories on, and I have no idea how she types on the thing so easily. I'd end up with gibberish if I gave up my laptop keyboard for a touchscreen. I watch her fingers move fast as she pulls up the *ScandalLust* site. Then she flicks the tablet my way like it's a Frisbee.

"Careful!" I say, catching it.

"Eh, it's under warranty. Plus, it's a company loan." She winks, and I look down at the page she's pulled up.

ScandalLust's flashy homepage is cluttered with ads and headlines and slideshows of photos. It's easy to pinpoint what she wanted to show me though. Right at the top of the page I see *"The Lust List: Check Out Our Newest Hottie"*, and right there, for all the Internet to see is a photo of Miles Riot on a stage, shirtless, with his guitar. My hunch was right—there are tattoos sprawled all over his chest. I thought of getting a tattoo once, but those things are forever. Miles, though, he doesn't seem to care what they'll look like when he's eighty. The ink trails over the hard lines of his chest and abs, dipping down past the waistline of his jeans. The muscles in his arms are taut and covered with a sheen of sweat as he plays for his audience. And he's looking up, his face clearly visible, unlike the show last night. His dark eyes gaze out toward the crowd and the grin on his face is both alluring and mischievous.

The rush of excitement that warms my body frightens me. This guy is not my type. No. Not at all. The way he acted last night— how he blew me off, how he hooked up with random strangers—it was unappealing, a little disgusting.

But my body betrays me as my heartbeat quickens and my hands get clammy. I listen to my pulse thunder in my ears as I click the link and read the next page.

Fresh from the L.A. night scene, Miles Riot is our next stud to watch. He's talented, beautiful...and single—just how we like them! This sexy guitarist is one-quarter of Vitriol, a rock band on the rise [complete with Kennedy Rose—Miles's younger sister—on vocals, Nate Camden on bass, and Dax Miller on drums]. The band is heading out on tour, so it's only a matter of time before the stunningly gorgeous Miles is scooped up by some lucky girl. Get 'em while you can!

My heartbeat hasn't settled as it dawns on me just how close I'll be to Miles for the next week. Working near him, eating near him, sleeping near him, showering near him. Every ounce of me wants to quit right now. I'll give my official notice to Jonathan, go back home to Texas, stay with my mom, find a simpler job.

"Are you awake over there?" Dee asks.

I look up at her. "I think I'm going to puke. I can't do this."

"Do what? You can definitely write a better story than *that*," she says, pointing to the tablet. "Plus, that guy really is hot. How can you say no to spending a week with him *while* getting paid?"

Hot? Miles? Tattoos, lip ring, and overdue for a haircut. "Maybe you should do it then."

Her mouth opens to say something before she changes her mind. I think she's catching on to my predicament. "You want him, don't you?"

"No. Absolutely not. He's...dirty...or something. He's not my type. It's just weird that I'm going to be spending all this time with him—with all of them, I mean."

"Mhmm. If you say so, but I'm not buying it. Part of your good girl, tiny town, healthy upbringing brain is wondering: what would it be like to get plowed by a rock star."

I chuck the closest pillow at her in response, then hear my phone ringing, grateful for the interruption. It's Eddie, the guy Jonathan went through to set this up.

"I'm out front," he tells me, and I panic. I'm not even done packing.

I scramble to my wardrobe, nearly knocking over my acoustic guitar, and grab the last of the things I need, the essentials. I scoop up a handful of panties and bras and shove the pile of lace and silk into my bag. In my bathroom, I snatch my packed toiletry bag, tossing it in, zipping it closed, and stepping into a pair of flats.

Chord watches me quizzically as I hug him. "I'll be back soon. You and Dee stay out of trouble."

I hug my friend and thank her again for helping me out.

As I leave, the door closing slowly behind me, I hear Dee say one last goodbye. "Let yourself go a little crazy."

I took the assignment, didn't I? I've already gone crazy.

*

When they said I'd be on a tour bus for a week, my stomach turned. I assumed a grungy, nearly broken down, oversized vehicle filled with trash and strange odors. I've seen buses and vans used by other bands that shouldn't be approached without donning a hazmat suit. Last night, when I got onto Vitriol's bus—and again just now—my mind was blown. This is high-end luxury. I've never seen anything like it. When you step on, your breath is taken away by the modern lines and the glow of LEDs imbedded in chrome rails overhead and in the floors under the furniture. The kitchen you first walk past is nicer than the one in my studio. It's like an optical illusion. From the outside, it's a cramped bus. Inside, the space grows and looks more like a luxury private jet than an oversized vehicle on half a dozen wheels. There are enough seats and couches to comfortably fit twice as many people than will be in it, and they're all plush, flawless gray leather. Everything is either wood or leather, and a silky curtain in the back leads to even more. Of course, I'm not sure what to make out of the shiny metal stripper pole in the middle of the lounge area. My cheeks flush with visions of naked girls and wild parties, but I shake it off. Just because it's an...amenity...doesn't mean it'll be used. The only thing missing...the band.

"Where is everyone?" I ask Eddie, who's taken a seat behind the steering wheel.

"It's only one o'clock. They're sleeping." He motions to the curtained off bunks. "Enjoy the quiet while you can." He points to one of the open bunks. "That's where you'll sleep. It doesn't look like much, but I assure you it's much more comfortable than you think. Like a personal cocoon. Next time my wife and I fight, I know where to go." He laughs like his marital issues are a common, insignificant occurrence. "There's room for your stuff up there too. The bathroom's in the back right before the main bedroom." He lowers his voice. "That's destined to be their fucking room, so stick to your loft when you need a nap or buy your own sheets, if you know what I mean."

Gross.

"We'll be in Vegas in about four hours. Make yourself comfortable and let me know if you need anything that's not already here."

"You're riding with us, right?" I ask. I'm not sure I can take on the whole band by myself.

"Hell no. I'll follow in my Benz. You've got Mark driving. You're in good hands."

I thank Eddie and move toward my designated loft. It's small, but it's nice to have something of my own. I pull my laptop out and shove my bag into the empty shelf at the end of the mattress.

Taking a seat in a lone chair by the refrigerator, I open my computer and open a text window to start taking notes.

Vitriol. National tour.

Need personal info on each band member.

Kennedy Rose

Miles Riot

Nate Camden

Dax Miller

Reference notes should be the easy part. It's my experiences and how I weave that into an entertaining story that'll be harder. I skip a couple lines and type two words that feel as if I'm sealing my fate.

Day One

*

My computer dings—an alert telling me I have a new message. I open the app and see it's Dee.

Dee: *How are things going?*

A moment to procrastinate. Thank God.

Me: *I've been staring at a screen for 15 minutes. No ideas.*

Dee: *That's because it just started. Nothing's happened yet, dummy.*

Movement catches the corner of my eye. The curtain on the right side loft in front of me slides open, and two tanned legs drop down. The rest of Nate follows and he slinks over to the kitchenette, ignoring me.

Me: *I should go. I'll keep you updated.*

Dee: *Better hook me up with backstage passes when y'all get back to LA.*

Nate opens the mini-fridge and pulls out a carton of juice, drinking from it, and returning it, before turning back to the couch and collapsing into it. He runs his hands over his face as if to wipe away his exhaustion and probable hangover, and then, as if he's just now waking up, he spots me.

"Oh hey." He looks out the window, squinting his eyes. "Where are we, Mark?" he calls to the driver.

"Still in L.A. We've barely begun this trip."

"Yeah, well, did you make sure it was clear of groupies before you started driving? Looks like you forgot to let one off." He looks back at me. "Who were you with last night? Dax?"

Is he serious? He met me last night—knows why I'm here. Or did he forget? "I'm Abby. I'm the journalist with Lydian, remember?"

"You let a fucking pap on the bus?" he yells at Mark.

"*Journalist*," I correct him, not bothering to conceal my irritation with the accusation. "Big difference."

"You go to college or something?" He leans back and plops his feet up on the table in front of him.

"I did. UT Austin. Summa cum lau—"

"Smart chicks." He grins, nodding his head slowly as he informs me, "I like smart chicks."

"Do us a favor and wait until we get to the hotel to screw her, okay?" Kennedy's emerged from the back bedroom. Her hair's in a messy knot on top of her head, and I'm surprised to see she's wearing flannel pajamas. This is far more ordinary of her than I'd have expected. "Don't let him bother you," she tells me with a smile that I eagerly return. I thank the stars Vitriol chose a female lead singer. Us girls have to stick together.

* * *

Miles

I hear Kennedy stumbling back toward the bedroom and pull open the curtain to tell her my big revelation of last night. After going down on Fire and taking Ice from behind, I had this epiphany.

Vitriol is a shitty band name.

We've already changed it four times, but if we're about to be signed, we have to have a name that can last decades. Fire and Ice were like a storm raging on an open sea. They were like riding a rollercoaster without a safety bar. It was wild and got me thinking—I think great during sex. A violent storm. Thrashing.

All these ideas are coming back to me as I climb out of the loft. Nate's already up, hitting on the reporter chick. I head to the liquor cabinet and find the bottle of vodka, pouring a shot into a lowball glass. I gulp that down and pour another, this time, grabbing the orange juice carton from the fridge behind me and topping off the glass. Breakfast.

Nate reaches for the vodka bottle and I hand it over as I tell him, "We need a band meeting. I've got an idea." I smack the last closed curtain of Dax's loft. "Get up, lazy ass." I call to the closed door in the back, "Kennedy. Out here."

It's clear they lack my enthusiasm, but I know they're listening.

I sit down next to Nate and relay my great idea. "We should use something like cyclone. Or typhoon. Make it sexy sounding somehow."

"Like Hurricane Descends," Nate offers. "Or, uh...Maelstrom Fury."

A voice from above us says, "Those are shit." Dax is up now. "Sound like elementary vocabulary lists. Nothing sexy about that."

"Tempest," I hear.

It's Abby, the journalist. What's she know about this? I open my mouth to tell her to butt out, but then... *Tempest.* Shit, I like it.

"Kennedy," I call again, but she doesn't respond. "Something Tempest. This can work." I start running through name ideas while the guys call out their own.

"Epic Tempest."

"Tempest Max."

"Tempest Ultra."

"High Tempest."

I stop them. "Wait, wait. Go back. That one was good. *Tempest Ultra.*"

Nate and Dax repeat it. Tempest Ultra.

Hell yeah. We did that quick.

"Tempest Ultra!" I hold up my glass and clink it against Nate's vodka bottle. Even reporter girl is happy, seeming a little too pleased with herself though. It's not like it was her idea.

Then Kennedy storms out of the room. "Stop the fucking bus!" she yells at Mark, while buttoning the last button on her shorts. She loops a belt around, fumbling and shaking.

"We're on a schedule, Kennedy," Mark tells her. "Unless it's an emergency—"

"It is." She's practically hyperventilating as she pulls her hair down and puts it back up. I've seen this side of my sister enough to know she's most likely being over dramatic. And it probably has to do with a guy.

"It can wait, Ken," I tell her.

"I can't breathe in here. I'm getting off this bus now, whether it's moving or not."

She moves to the door, but I stand up and quickly get between her and her suicide mission. "Pull over, Mark." I glare down at Kennedy as I talk to Mark. "She'll make this quick."

No sooner than we stop, Kennedy jumps off the bus and starts pacing down the L.A. highway. The rest of us stay back to let her get it out of her system. She's got to choose her boyfriends better, and unfortunately, the current one has the power to bring us all down.

"Is she okay?" Abby asks, again butting in where she has no right.

"She'll be fine." I take this woman in again. Nice body. Sweet face. A kind demeanor. She's got no business hanging out in this scene. She'll be eaten alive. I almost feel bad for her.

Eddie storms onto the bus. "We gotta go, you guys." Eddie's annoyed, but he should be used to this by now. Kennedy's impulsive, emotional, stubborn. It makes her great on stage but a pain in the ass behind the scenes. I should know, I've known her her entire life.

"I'll go get her," I volunteer, because no one else will. It's always big brother to the rescue.

I follow down the freeway until I catch up to her. "Where do you plan on going?" I ask.

She's crying and looks like she's ready to scream. "Devon's."

See? Told you it was boyfriend problems. "And you're going to walk the whole way there? Then what?"

She swings around toward me. "The fucker waited until I got on the road to dump me. No, not just dump me, but rip my heart out. He says he was with some slut last night. And the night before. Fuck him."

"Well, you can't murder Devon Stone. Not when there's a chance Stone Records is going to sign us. So let's get back on the road and get out of California."

She doesn't hear a word I say. "I'll show him. I'll slash every tire of his precious car. Or sink his fucking yacht."

I turn and see Eddie waiting outside of the bus, his arms up in the air as if I didn't already know this was inconveniencing the asshole. I signal for them to drive down this way. "You know what? Let's see who offers us a contract first. If and when the Stone label is off the table, you can do anything you want to him." I don't like the guy anyway. He and Kennedy are always doing this. They cheat on each other and break up. They screw each other and make up. It's been a nonstop cycle for almost a year. But it's just one more toxic element to this life, and at least I'm around to make sure Kennedy doesn't do anything truly stupid.

Our entourage pulls up closer and I push Kennedy toward the still open door. "By the way," I tell her, "we changed the band name."

Chapter Three

Abby

All the way to Vegas, I sat back and listened, learning a wealth of information about this band. Kennedy is—was—dating Devon Stone, billionaire heir to Stone Records. Nate has been in and out of rehab for drugs and alcohol, but has yet to sober up. Dax is actually nice *when* he chooses to be. The rest of him seems to run on a spectrum between silent and violent. And Miles...Well, Miles is the most mysterious. The vibe I get tells me he worries more about everyone else than himself. He's a workaholic who considers liquor a food group. Of everyone, he'll be the hardest shell to crack if I plan on writing a story that digs into who they are on a personal level.

The Vegas show is sold out, and we see the line already wrapping around the building as we pull up. The show doesn't even start for another couple hours. I hang out backstage watching the setup and sound check. For all the drama I've seen on the road in one day, it amazes me how they all switch gears when they need to be Vitriol—I mean, Tempest Ultra. Maybe I need to include that in my story. How do they keep so many fans when they can't commit to a band name?

From the first note to the last, the audience is wild. This venue is much better than the sleazy bar from last night. The stage is ten times as big—as is the crowd. And the energy emanating off everyone seems to charge the space with electricity. Kennedy, no longer on a cramped square of a stage, uses her space to seduce her fans. She jumps down closer to the front row, singing inches away from people's faces. Then, in the first break in the lyrics, she grabs the closest man—mid-twenties, shaved head, dark skin—and plants a kiss on his lips before jumping back on stage and not missing a beat.

I check out her brother's reaction to Kennedy's flirtation with promiscuity, but Miles keeps his head down, focused more on his guitar. His hands, wearing black fingerless gloves tonight, move fast over the strings, and I snap myself away from him before I let my eyes linger too long on the silhouette of his hard chest underneath his tight black shirt.

The story, Abby. I can do something about family—the sibling bond between Miles and Kennedy, and how he's Mr. Protective Big Brother until showtime, when he refuses eye contact with his sister in order to avoid seeing how she behaves in front of thousands of strangers. But hey, it's show business, and even he must understand sex sells. He was so protective of her earlier, coaxing her back to the bus. Once we were driving again, he and Kennedy disappeared to talk in the back room, and by the time she reappeared, her mood had improved entirely. Not even my own sister and I can patch things up for each other so quickly. Of course, in order to follow this story idea, I'd have to spend a whole lot more time with this mysterious rock star. The flutter in my chest is the first warning sign that it's a bad idea. I'll find another spin.

By the time the show's over, my ears are ringing. At least backstage access prevented any more mishaps with mosh pits. As the roadies rush past me to start collecting the gear, I find myself feeling useless.

"Can I help with anything?" I ask one of them.

"Who the hell are you?" He looks at me like I'm an unwelcome fan who snuck back here.

"I'm—"

"She's Abby. Don't be rude," Miles says from behind. "She's with us."

The roadie shrugs and keeps working.

I turn to Miles. "Thanks." That was...unexpected.

"It's nothing."

"I really don't mind helping if you—"

"I wouldn't want you to hurt any of your writing fingers carrying things."

Oh, so he wants to be a smartass? "It's no worse than you hurting your strumming fingers." Surprise flashes across his face for a split second. He's not the only one with the quick wit.

Instead of trying to one-up me, he picks up his guitar and walks off, leaving me standing there alone. And leave it to my own mind's betrayal, I find myself feeling disappointed.

*

The bus seemed much bigger hours ago. Now, it's packed with the band, Eddie, myself, and an array of half-naked women. Why are these the ones the guys choose to take home? Don't they have standards?

One of the girls straddles Nate on the couch, gyrating into his hips, paying no attention to all these witnesses of her pornographic display. Nate doesn't seem to mind either as one hand trails up the back of her sheer top and the other fumbles around at the hem of her miniskirt. I'm slightly disgusted but also...intrigued. I like sex just as much as the next person, but it's a private thing. It's meant to be behind closed doors, an intimate moment between two people. So what would it be like to be so open? To not care about who sees?

The thought alone makes me uncomfortable. No way. To each their own, I'll say. Dax sits next to the grinding duo, drinking a steady line of shots. Judging by the liquor supply, it looks like Eddie restocked during the show. He offers a bottle of tequila to Kennedy, who takes it without hesitation. Then

Dax runs his hand along the neck of the woman on top of Nate. She stops for a second to look over at him, and Dax leans over, crushing his mouth into hers. I see more than enough tongue action to expect Nate to flip out. But he laughs, and when Dax is done kissing his girl, Nate pulls her up to standing and leads her into the back room. The empty space next to Dax quickly fills with two more fan girls ready to find out how their luck will play out tonight.

Kennedy hands the tequila bottle to Miles, who takes a swig and hands it to me.

This completely catches me off guard, but it was probably a mistake. There are so many people, he was most likely just passing it to the nearest empty hand.

"Thanks, but I'll pass," I say and try to hand it back.

"Drink. Relax." He smiles a mischievous grin, and dammit, that same warmth drives its way through me. "We had a great show.

Now we're off to the after party. Put your work away and chill a little."

Those were the most words he's exchanged with me since we met. I tip the bottle up, filling my mouth with the liquid that instantly burns. I hold back my reflex to choke and let the liquor become my excuse for feeling so...hot.

Over the next twenty minutes, Mark drives while everyone gets ready for a night off. The volume level in the not-so-private back room increases with moans and banging sounds. I try to drown it out. My cheeks burn from the embarrassment on their behalf, but no one else on this bus pays any attention. You'd think I was the only one who could hear them, but it doesn't take superhero-strength auditory senses to recognize the exact moment Nate makes his mystery woman orgasm. There's a slight chuckle from Dax, and I try to hide just how appalled I am. Then it's like nothing ever happened when Nate comes out of the room a few minutes later dressed in a suit. I'm caught off guard by how well he's cleaned up—like one man went in and another came out. He sits, and his girl of the night takes a seat on his lap, her eyes heavy and smile permanent. Kennedy disappears next, returning in a fiery red dress that leaves little to the imagination. Dax skips the privacy of the room and changes in the middle of everyone. Shirtless Dax makes the horny girls swoon, but once he drops his pants, I avert my eyes and take that as my cue to change into something nicer. Standing on tiptoes, I dig through my bag, thankful I packed a little black dress. I pair it with white heels for some personality and turn to go into the bathroom.

"You can use the room." Miles is behind me. What's with him sneaking up like that? Second time now. "It's bigger."

And has had a lot of unmentionable things happen in it in a very short time. "I'm okay. Thank you."

"Suit yourself." He takes the room, while I squeeze into the bathroom.

Alone, I close my eyes and take a deep breath. The tequila's made me tipsy and the proximity to all this—the noise, the sex, the temptations, the glamour—I can't help but feel...not like myself at all. Right now, I don't want to be the small town, sweet girl. I want to be one of those girls out there. One of the shameless groupies who are liberated enough to practically have sex in front of strangers. Impulsive. Sexual. *Sexy.*

I want to break free.

What the hell is wrong with me?

*

What's a night in Vegas without a fancy casino? The bus pulls up to the front of the Vernazza Hotel and Casino and we all pile out. Now I'm really grateful for the alcohol. My mind's less cluttered with assignment-related thoughts, and I'm not even bothered by the bystanders crowding around to see what important people just showed up. They spot Kennedy first and get excited, and then Miles suddenly has a new woman on each arm. Dax and Nate follow with their groupies, and Eddie and I trail the band.

"Is it always like this?" I ask him.

He laughs. "They're rising stars. Ever since they got that first whiff of celebrity status, they've been eating it up. But they're good at what they do, so who am I to tell them who they should fuck?"

Well, when you put it that bluntly. "I just can't imagine managing them. Is it stressful?"

"My bank account hasn't been stressed, so neither am I." He winks. I can't decide if he's a creep or just a cocky ass. "Besides, they're easier than other acts I've managed. Heard of Bia?"

The internationally famed pop star? *Everyone's* heard of Bia. She's got multi-platinum *and* diamond records, all her singles have hit the Top 10, and she's collaborated with a ton of big names. "Yeah, I've heard of her." I can't believe he managed Bia too.

"Well, she has a sister whose friend was trying to hit it big." Yep, that makes much more sense and seems to be more on Eddie's level. Working with Tempest is his closest chance to making his career, as long as the band doesn't take a nosedive in the next few weeks. He's still talking about the someone who knows someone who knows Bia. "Didn't work out for her, but my god. That bitch wanted everything handed to her from sunrise to sunset. At least with these guys, I just have to get them from one place to the next without losing any of them in the process. It's like herding sheep."

Nice. The guy who hopes to get rich off Tempest Ultra just referred to them as livestock. I nod my head politely, but the second we're inside the Vernazza, I pick a direction and wander away from the group. I need to recharge and this gorgeous casino is dazzling enough to keep my mind off the absurdity of my current situation. The casino foyer opens into an enormous ballroom filled with game tables and slot machines. So many chances to lose money in one space, but people are having fun. It's loud with cheers and conversation.

"Can I get you a drink?" a server wearing a black tux asks me.

"White wine, please."

And he rushes off, only to find me a minute later, a wine glass in his hand.

"Add that to Ed's tab, okay?" I hear someone say behind me. It's Miles, surprising me again.

"You lost your female accessories," I quip, picking up the same sarcastic tone from earlier.

The corners of his lips turn up. "And you seem to have lost the party. VIP's up there." He nods his head, motioning towards upstairs.

I could stay down here, people watch, and maybe even catch the open mic show later. Or I can follow Miles up to the band's after party, letting the unexpected happen. I know better

than this. I should keep to myself. Stay professional.

But one second of letting Miles look me
straight in the eye—those intense chocolate
brown orbs staring into me, and I'm done for.
I've got his attention. And I want to keep it.
"After you."

* * *

Miles

I don't know what to think of this chick, but
tonight, the other girls just aren't doing it for
me. A full day on the road, and Abby hasn't
tried to fuck me. This makes her instantly in-
triguing. Either she's gay or she takes her job
far too seriously. Whichever it is, I'm up for
the challenge.

We reach a winding staircase, and like a
gentleman, I step aside to let her go first. Her
tight black dress hugs her curves, and with
each step her hips taunt me. My eyes are

glued to her ass, and the urge to sink my teeth into that sweet, professional flesh is strong.

Upstairs is just as crowded as the main floor. I press the palm of my hand against the small of Abby's back, leading her toward the VIP lounge. She doesn't push my hand away. I smile to myself. Most of the women I sleep with are easy—hot and ready when I finish a show. I just have to pick one out, like I'm shopping. Fucking the reporter will be a nice change of pace.

Tonight, Abby. Tomorrow night...well, your guess is as good as mine.

I get us past the VIP line and the doors open for us, inviting us into one hell of a party.

"Wow," Abby says as she takes in the room. Floor-to-ceiling, sheer curtains separate several plush, curved sofas. This isn't the table and bar stool type of place. Leather couches with low, wooden tables and the false sense of privacy from those curtains give guests their own space while the raised dance floor shows off an orgy of bodies moving to the same beat. The deejay'll play anything we want in here, and tonight Tempest Ultra calls the shots. It's our fucking night.

The band's in the corner. The guys are surrounded by sexy women, and Kennedy's got some waiter flirting with her. I gesture for Abby to sit, and she slides in next to Dax.

"Hey man." I nudge the waiter. He's wasting his time if he thinks Kennedy will be interested. "How about a round of shots? Bourbon. Then a second bourbon on the rocks." I look down at Abby. "What else you want?"

"Um, a cosmo. Please."

Such a chick drink. "And a cosmo for the lady." The waiter wanders off, and I sit down next to Abby, extending my arm across the back of the couch behind her head. Now to reel her in for the catch.

Kennedy and Nate are talking about tomorrow's plans once we get to Tucson. Dax's girl has him distracted, her hands happily massaging their way up his legs.

"So, where are you from?" I ask Abby.

"Texas."

"A Southern girl." Explains the manners. "How'd you end up in L.A.?" The waiter's back with our drinks. He sets down the cosmo and then lines up the shots in front of all of us. "Oh, wait."

I stand up and get everyone to shut up and pay attention. "Good show tonight," I start, yelling over the music, loud enough that everyone nearby stops to listen. "Keep it up, and we'll be rich motherfuckers by August!"

Cheers all around as we down the shots. Even Abby plays along. Someone behind me grabs my shoulders. I turn around, but before I can see who it is, plump, fake lips meet mine and a hand tries to work its way down to my crotch.

"Hey now." I move the assaulter back a step. A woman with straight black hair and a dress made out of lace smiles back at me.

"Congratulations on a successful night. Can I help you celebrate?" Damn, she's hot. But I've already set my goal for the night.

"Maybe another time, babe. I'm busy."

She fakes disappointment looking up at me with big doe eyes. "You're missing out," she taunts me.

I believe her too. Something tells me she's quite the giver in bed. "I'm sure." But then I turn away and sit back down next to Abby.

"You're popular," she says, smiling. I see half her cosmo is gone.

"Goes with the job." I drink my bourbon and ask her again how she ended up in Los Angeles.

"After school, I applied for every reliable entertainment magazine in the U.S. Lydian wasn't my first pick, but they hired me. I wasn't going to turn it down, so I moved to L.A."

"Sounds like you didn't want to."

"Definitely wasn't my first choice," she says, taking another sip of her drink. I wave the waiter over to bring us another round.

Sweet, Southern woman moves to the city of cutthroat entertainment. You either do your job better than everyone else, or you get replaced in a heartbeat. I don't know this woman, but Abby doesn't seem like the type who plays dirty—unfortunately.

She takes a second to look around. I notice Cylon Smash just came in. Landers Thompson, their bass player, is an old buddy of mine and I call him over.

"There you are," he says, slapping me on the back. "Heard you've got Stone and Rev Records fighting over you. Nice work."

"Natural talent, man," I say, laughing. Cylon's spent years trying to get signed, but hadn't hit the jackpot yet. We've been fucking around just as long, sure, but once we got serious and started sending out the demos, the labels started calling us.

"Uh huh. Natural talent is the Mr. Smoldering face you've got plastered all over the tabloids. Better watch yourself. You'll fall quickly to teen sex symbol if you let them keep it up."

I shudder at the thought of a bunch of underage girls filling the concert venues. I'll have to start checking IDs before I sleep with any of them.

Abby's laughing and Kennedy's joined in.

"Like you're one to talk, Landers. I was barely legal when we—"

"Whoa, whoa," I break in. "No need to make me sick." I try to forget who Kennedy's hooked up with. Sure, she's an adult and can do her own thing, but I don't want to hear about it.

Kennedy laughs and turns to Abby, her sly smile on her face. That's the look she's got when she's up to no good. "How about you, Dear Abby? You're eighteen, right?"

"Twenty-three, actually, but I'm no groupie." She looks over at me. "Sorry."

Oh, so she's taking some blows too? Fair enough. A vague rejection's never stopped me. I can charm the panties off anyone. She'll see.

Kennedy rolls her eyes at Abby. "Right." Then she stands up and lures Landers toward the dance floor.

I finish my drink and start on the next.

"My turn to ask the questions," Abby says. "Why'd you start a band with your sister?"

"Oh no. I know better than to answer questions from a reporter. That's dangerous ground." I turn the subject back on her. "What would've been your first choice, if not L.A.?"

"Staying close to home. I miss my family and all my old friends."

That's almost too sweet to handle. "So you hate L.A. that much?"

"It's just...not my taste."

"The clubs? The parties?" I coax her. What's not to love about a city with access to everything anytime? There's always somewhere to be, someone to hook up with. You can keep busy.

"Not my taste," she says again, this time smiling a cute, flirty smile. Groupie, my ass. She's totally into me.

"The music. Tempest Ultra," I say with a smirk. I know I've got her this time. She's already proved her love of the industry.

"Not...my...taste," she answers slowly, drunkenly. Her eyes go wide as she realizes what she's just said out loud.

"What the fuck? Wait. You can't tell me you aren't into Tempest. You're lying."

She shakes her head and bursts into a fit of giggles. I wait for her to compose herself, but instead of apologizing, she says, "It's true." Still laughing, she explains too honestly, "I tried to get out of this assignment. I told my boss anyone else would be better for it. But there was no way out." Tears fill her eyes as she fights to catch her breath through her laughter. So...alcohol makes her brutally honest and puts her into hysterics. I won't lie. I'm deeply amused. And a little offended.

"So the journalist writing a story about Tempest...*hates* Tempest?" I drink my bourbon as I let the thought sit between us for a second. "This'll work out well."

Chapter Four

Abby

I feel like I can't control myself, but all the
ridiculousness of this day has caught up to me
and at this point, there's no turning back.
"Sorry. I shouldn't have said all that."

Now it's Miles's turn to laugh. "You kidding? You just made this week infinitely more
exciting. So you really aren't a groupie?" He
nods slowly as though he's accepting the
revelation.

"What? Did you think you were going to sleep with me or something?"

"No," he answers bluntly, and it's a little painful. Not that I wanted to, but as promiscuous as he seems to be, it's a blow to my ego that he wouldn't even entertain the thought. What do those other girls have that I don't—except way less dignity? "I prefer women who like my music."

"Why? Do they scream out your song lyrics in bed or something?"

Dammit, cosmopolitans. You've killed off my filter. Alcohol's like a truth serum, and I don't think before blurting things out.

Miles smiles. "Damn, I wish they did. That might be hot."

I shake my head.

The guy from earlier shows back up at the table and plops down in Kennedy's seat. "Got cock blocked by your sister's boyfriend," he says to Miles, shaking his head in fake disappointment. What's with these rock stars?

What, do they have a quota to meet each night?

Landers turns and starts talking to Nate about a new Cylon Smash single they're recording, but Miles interrupts him. "My sister's boyfriend?"

"Yeah, that Stone douche showed up right as I thought I'd have a chance with her."

"Fuck. Where'd they go?" Miles stands up.

"The balcony," Landers answers, his eyebrows raised. Miles hurries off without another word.

My curiosity gets the best of me, and I follow. "What's wrong?" I ask once I catch up.

"He broke up with Kennedy today. That's why she spazzed earlier." He weaves through the dance floor toward the large glass doors on the other side.

He pushes through, and a gust of cool, night air has a sobering effect on me. Miles surveys the space, which is quieter and much emptier. I spot Kennedy on the other side, sitting in a lounge chair with a guy on top of her. Really, it's her bright hair that gives her away. Miles must see her too because he charges over there.

"Let's get out of here, Kennedy," he says, interrupting the two's make out session.

The guy looks up, and I realize this is the closest I've ever been to Devon Stone. The Stone family is notorious. They seem to run all of L.A. Between their enormously successful, international record label and the entertainment law firm they manage, everyone knows who the Stones are. Very few get close access to them. In fact, it's impossible for people like me to get into their lavish parties, and they don't take interviews unless they're the ones who set it up—and that's all carefully construed through their P.R. rep.

But here's Devon Stone. Right here. You think *ScandalLust* had fun announcing Miles on their Lust List? They put Devon on it every chance they get. He sits up and eyes Miles with blatant disdain. "What did you just say?"

"I told my sister it's time to go."

Devon looks back at Kennedy, nuzzling his face into her neck. He kisses her, and she moans, closing her eyes. His hand trails down her arm and over to her hips. "You want to leave, baby?" he asks her.

"Only with you," she says in a daze.

That's when I notice the little table next to their chair. On it, a little blue tin lays open, revealing a folded bag of white powder inside. The table itself has a line of powdery dust, and I quickly put it all together.

Devon's messy hair and five o'clock shadow, combined with his icy blue eyes, gives off this air of intensity. He's intimidating. He's gorgeous. He's powerful.

And he's high on cocaine. I think it's safe to assume Kennedy's had her own share.

I'm certain Miles knows this too, but he's not completely freaked out by it, which is what I'd be if I caught my sister like this.

"Kennedy." Miles's tone switches from suggestive to authoritative. "A few hours ago, Devon dumped you. You were ready to kill him." I hear Devon laugh as Miles continues. "You need to stay away from him."

Miles grabs Kennedy's arm and pulls her to standing. She resists, but she's unstable and too high to put up a fight.

Devon stands up and gets in Miles's face. "How 'bout you back off? She can take care of herself."

Not right now, she can't. Kennedy can barely stand without support, and the second Miles lets go of her to inch closer to Devon, she collapses back down on the lounge chair, giggling.

Miles pushes Devon back. "Listen, man. I'm trying to be nice. You two need to leave each other alone. Ken's got a career to build. She can't keep playing your games, and you've proven time and time again you don't actually want her."

"You don't know what I want, shmuck." This time, it's Devon pushing back. He slams a hand into Miles's chest, but Miles hardly reacts. "And who do you think is fucking building your career? Mess with me. Go ahead and try. And you'll never see a Stone contract. I'll ruin you. Want to test me?"

Devon's eyes are threatening—glazed over from drugs, burning with rage. But Miles stands tall, shoulders held back, jaw clenched. On the stage, he comes across as the sexy loner—yes, fine, I admit he's sexy. But when he's performing, he gives this impression of solitude, like he's the outsider who sticks to himself.

But right now...right now, he's Mr. Alpha, standing firm, unrelenting. Devon doesn't scare him—at least, he doesn't show it. Which is great, because Devon Stone scares the crap out of me.

Then Miles throws the first punch. It's unexpected, and Devon takes the full force of his fist to the side of his face. Kennedy shrieks and pushes herself to standing, like she's going to intervene. I stand speechless. *This isn't how you handle a conflict,* I want to yell at him.

But Devon lunges. He punches Miles in the jaw and his hand finds Miles's throat. He pushes him backward as he threatens him. "Don't fuck with me, asshole. I'll do so much worse than destroy your career. I'll fucking kill you." Onlookers stop their conversations and form a semi-circle around us, watching and whispering. Their shocked faces are more intrigued with suspense than they are horrified by the fight. No one does anything to break it up, but a few pull out their phones and start snapping pictures. Classy.

"You do realize...dickhead," Miles chokes out his words, his airway being cut off by Devon, "whatever you do...to me...affects her." He lifts his arm up and points toward Kennedy. "So leave her alone...Find someone else. No more of this shit."

Now Devon's got Miles against the rail of the balcony. The top of it digs into his back as Devon pushes him further, bending Miles's upper body back, his shoulders and head dangling over a drop that would kill him if Devon flipped him over the rail. My heart pounds. I have to do something.

"Stop," I shout to no avail. "It's not worth it, guys. Come on!"

I try to wedge myself between Miles and Devon and smell a mix of liquor and cologne on them both. Kennedy's next to us, and I can't tell whose side she's on. Devon pauses for a second to look at me, and Miles takes the opportunity to shove Devon back, knocking him onto the ground. Miles moves away from the rail, rubbing his throat with one hand, clenching his fist with the other. A trail of blood spills from the cut on his mouth, staining his lip ring.

"And who are you?" Devon asks me as he gets up. Kennedy wraps her arms around him, clearly not concerned about what just happened to her brother. "His bodyguard? He *would* need a woman to take care of him."

"Judging by your swollen eye, it looks like Miles can take care of himself." I can't believe I just said that, and I instantly regret it. Devon's eyes blaze with fury, this time focused on me.

"Bitch. You two are perfect together." Devon looks from me, to Miles, and back at me. "Rot in hell." He wraps his arm around Kennedy's lower back, his hand planted on her butt. "Let's go."

They walk away, hanging on to each other like a drunk couple in love. How can Kennedy be okay with that? Her brother tries to protect her, yet she goes with the guy who could've killed him just now? She's clearly never heard of family loyalty.

* * *

Miles

That wasn't my first fight with Devon Stone. It probably won't be the last. Not until Kennedy learns.

"You okay?" Abby asks me. For a second, I'm pissed she followed me out here. It's not her business. Nor is it the business of any of the assholes still staring our way.

But she tried to help, and who knows? If it wasn't for her, there's a chance Devon would've thrown me over the edge of the balcony. He stays so drugged up all the time, I doubt he would've thought anything of it. And his rich dad would've paid his way out of the legal trouble. Not that I know of any murders in the Stone family, but they've gotten away with everything else.

"I'm fine," I tell Abby, pushing through the nosy crowd and going back inside.

"You're bleeding," she says, keeping pace with me.

"It's nothing."

"You might need stitches."

"That's not your concern," I shoot back. Fuck. I just want to be left alone.

Abby follows me all the way back to the suite Eddie booked us. Maybe she'll take the hint when I lock my bedroom door. The mini bar in my room better be stocked well. We get to the suite, not saying another word, and I find a bottle of vodka. I swish a mouthful around, spitting it out into the sink. Alcohol kills germs or something, right? I take in another mouthful and swallow it this time. There we go. I just need to be more drunk. Enough liquor in me, and I won't give a shit what Kennedy decides to do. I'm so sick of taking care of her.

"Here," Abby says—yeah, she's still around—and now she's holding a towel filled with ice.

"Don't need it."

She rolls her eyes. "Oh my god. Suck it up, shut up, and let someone help you. You really think you'll be able to sing well tomorrow night if your lip's all swollen and puffy?"

I can't help but smile. *Yes, ma'am, Texas girl.*

"Take out your lip ring," she tells me, and I do it, pulling it out and dropping it onto the countertop. The hole burns with pain. I'm going to be pissed if that fucker ripped it.

I sit on a bar stool and let her press the ice against my mouth. I wince. "Fuck, that hurts."

She laughs. "I'm sure it does."

After a minute, I find my eyes wandering. As my own anger subsides, I notice the neckline of her dress. It scoops down over her round breasts, showing off a hint of cleavage. Kind of sexy. Her hair's a natural blond, and if I had my guess, I'd say she doesn't bother dying it. It circles around in curly ringlets, and I hold back the urge to run my fingers through it.

My dizzy mind sways as the liquor kicks back in. Oh, sweet intoxication. I'm feeling better already.

Abby's ears are pierced, a little diamond stud in each. There's no sign of any other piercing, or a tattoo, or any hint of some rebellious phase in her past. I'm being nurtured by a good girl.

"What's so funny?"

My expression must have given me away. I shake my head. "It's nothing." I change the subject. "Sorry he insulted you. Devon's an asshole."

"I've heard worse," she says. And she really doesn't seem to care. Good for her, not taking it personally. Other women I've known would've held on to that resentment, going on and on about how hurt they were, and making it all about them. Abby's not like other women.

She leans closer, reaching past me for a paper towel. My eyes involuntarily close as I breathe her in. She smells sweet and citrusy, like summertime on the beach. A change of pace from the norm—the smell of smoke and beer doused in excessive perfume.

Gently, she dabs the paper towel over my lip, cleaning the aftermath of the fight. Her hand brushes against my skin—soft, light. I turn to kiss it, but stop short. What the hell's happening?

She's not my type. But I did set a goal for the night to bang the reporter. Maybe this doctor-patient thing turns her on. I reach up with one arm and run my hand down her shoulder. My fingers graze the bare skin of her arm. Our eyes meet. I grin and it hurts like hell. I watch her chest rise and fall as she takes a deep breath. Yeah, this bad boy thing turns her on. There's no way around it, whether she likes my music or not. *Not her taste...* She's yet to take her first bite, is all. I'll show her.

My hands find her hips, and she lets me keep them there for a second before clearing her throat and taking a step back.

"Just keep it clean, and you should be fine." She hands the ice back to me. "It's late. I'll see you all in the morning."

She spins around and hurries to her room, closing the door behind her. Something spooked her. Do I scare her? Or is she really not interested?

Nah, I've yet to meet a woman who wasn't a fan of Miles Riot, and something tells me our fun has only just started.

Chapter Five

Abby

Easily, the best part of this job is the silence that exists in the early hours of the day. While the band sleeps off their night's exploitations, snoozing away their hangovers, I have this entire, beautiful suite to myself. I wonder if these guys know how close they are to fame when this is where they're set up for one night on tour. They must know most bands don't live this sort of luxury when they're trying to get signed. That guy last night—Landers—brought up how Stone and Rev Records are fighting over Tempest Ultra, and looking around this place, I'd guess it was Stone who paid for the accommodations.

Aside from the six guest rooms, this main living space is a bachelor's dream. One wall is lined with a full-size, two-lane bowling alley, and next to it, a pool table, foosball table, and an air hockey table. It's the kind of recreation you know brings out a man's inner ten year old. Sectional couches and an enormous flat screen TV take up the middle of the main space. Then there's the kitchen in one corner and a jacuzzi that could easily fit a dozen people in the other. None of this stuff looks like it was touched last night, which tells me all the partying took place downstairs. If I've learned anything from my co-workers' experiences with rock bands, it's that ninety-nine percent of hotel rooms don't stand a chance lasting a night with them. This suite managed to be in the lucky one percent.

I sit at the same bar stool Miles sat in last night, the counter cleaned and sanitized by yours truly, and my computer propped open, still staring at the bare page of notes I'd started on the bus. I already felt clueless about what I'd write, and now I'm even more confused.

What happened last night?

One moment, I was helping Miles after his bloody brawl with Devon Stone. The next moment, he's got his hands on me, looking at me with this expression that said...What did it say? He was messing with me. He had to have been. With his reputation for hooking up with a different woman every night, I must have been his last act of desperation—the only woman in the room.

But that moment, his hand touching my arm, my hip. It'd sent an electric shock to my core, and it was only a split second of common sense that snapped me out of it. Otherwise...I don't know what would've happened.

A door opens to my left, and I keep my eyes on the computer screen, not ready to interact with hungover rock stars just yet.

"It's like a cave in here," Kennedy says behind me.

I glance over my shoulder as she pushes a button on the wall and the wall-to-wall curtains slide open revealing a wall of glass overlooking the Vegas morning.

"That's better," Kennedy says with a smile. "How was your night?"

I do a quick survey of the room. There's no one else in here. She's definitely talking to me.

"All right," I say with trepidation. "And yours?"

She removes her robe, stripping down to just a bikini, and steps into the bubbling hot tub. "I had a phenomenal night," she says dreamily.

Does she not remember her night?

Then the same door opens a second time, and my throat catches. Devon Stone walks out.

Oh no. The drama of last night is only going to carry on to today. Let's hope we hit the road soon. Very soon.

Devon walks over to the kitchen and helps himself in the fridge. He turns around with a glass of ice water and watches Kennedy with the satisfaction of an adoring boyfriend. Then he places his glass down and notices me.

He nods. "Hey."

"Hi." My meek voice gives away my fear of this whole situation.

"Never seen a groupie who brings her work along with her." He smiles and walks around the countertop, taking a seat in the stool next to me, his back to the counter.

"Actually, I'm *not* a groupie. I'm a writer," I correct him. I'm also the girl you told to rot in hell last night...

He smirks. "What's a writer doing on tour with a rock band?"

"Writing."

"Oh, she's feisty," he says to no one in particular. "How about you put that work away and relax a little." He nods toward the hot tub. "You can join Kennedy, and if you're lucky, maybe I'll get in too."

This is the same guy who called me a bitch last night, but yeah, let me just dive into the hot tub and chill with a guy who's got no recollection of what happened twelve hours ago. Now I'm hoping it's the same for Miles. How drunk did he get last night? Clearly drunk enough to suddenly be interested in me. Maybe he won't remember the fight either.

A door opens and startles me. I'm not ready to find out right this second whether or not Miles is going to lash out at Devon. But it's Nate, and I exhale with relief.

"Good morning beautiful," Nate says to me just as a half-naked woman emerges from his room. She disappears into the bathroom and comes out a minute later dressed in last night's clothes.

Nate rummages through the kitchen while I go back to being preoccupied with my work. In other words, I have no idea how to react to any of these people right now, so I'm going to pretend to be busy. It works for all of two seconds before Miles walks in, and I leap out of my seat, closing my computer, prepared to rush to my room at the first sign of conflict. Or...do I stay?

This could be the story I need. It's almost too perfect. *Up-and-coming band can smell the record deal, but a personal feud between record executive and bandmate ruins everything.*

Only Devon seems to notice my internal battle. Do I report gossip that'll definitely please my boss? Or do I let their personal lives remain private, finding another story to tell?

Devon looks at me quizzically but I break eye contact and look at Miles. Yeah, Miles definitely remembers last night. He takes one look at Kennedy in the hot tub, one look at Devon sitting near me, and stomps out of the suite. I drop off my laptop in my room and rush after him, catching up to him in the hallway right before the elevator.

"Hey, hey! Hold up." I watch as he nearly slams his fist into the wall, stopping short of impact, and then dropping his clenched hands to his sides. "You okay?"

"I'm fine." He punches his finger into the elevator button.

"Oh yeah, I can tell." I follow him into the elevator only realizing after the doors close that I don't have a plan. What am I doing? Did I chase after him for my job? Or for another reason? No, no. This is a work obligation. Period. "Can I ask you something?"

He doesn't say anything. Instead, he looks over at me as the elevator makes its way down, and I feel the heat of his glare blazing through me. He's waiting for me to speak.

"Why do you worry about who your sister dates?"

He smirks and shakes his head, looking away from me. "I told you I don't talk to reporters."

"I'm not asking as a reporter."

I see his eyebrow raise as he reaches over and hits the emergency stop button on the elevator. We jolt to a halt. Miles comes closer to me, standing close enough I can smell him. He took a shower this morning and smells like whatever woodsy soap he uses. It's probably just hotel stuff, but mixed with his own scent, it's a little...intoxicating.

"What are you asking me as then, Abby?"

He steps another inch closer to me, but I instinctually back up, pressing myself into the elevator wall. "I don't know. I'm not going to throw the term 'friend' around, but I thought maybe you needed someone to talk to. I was there last night, and today, Kennedy and Devon are acting like nothing ever happened. For a second, I thought I'd hallucinated last night's fight."

This close to Miles, there's no easy way to look away from him. Yet, *this close to Miles*, it's blindingly obvious he's far more attractive than just the bad boy look he hides behind. The angles of his jawline, the even scruff of facial hair, his intense eyes that give away his true feelings. He could give up his music career and get rich as a model. Even *Scandal-Lust* called that one. But I'm seeing something else. There's more to him than he lets on. It's like he needs to be heard—is waiting to be heard—but has yet to have the real him acknowledged. There's hidden passion behind those eyes, and he conceals it by being just another hard-ass rock star who's only looking to get laid.

And if it's not already obvious, his hand reaching up to graze the side of my face proves my point.

"Why are you worried about me and my sister, *friend?*" He doesn't say it as a condescending remark. Instead, he's flirting, seeing what sort of boundaries he can push. I've always prided myself on being intuitive, and the signals I get from Miles are big, bold, and unmistakable.

"Why do you dodge my questions?" I ask in retaliation.

"I already told you. I don't give away my private life to reporters."

"And if I wasn't a reporter? If I was just trying to be nice? Then what would you do?"

"This." He smirks and leans in, crushing his mouth into mine.

His lips are hot and smooth, and I fight to catch my own breath and make sense of this. My hands slowly make their way to his chest—his firm, muscular chest—and my head spins. Miles reaches around me, pressing his hands to my lower back and pulling me closer to him. I get it. I get why the groupies lunge at him. He looks good. He smells good. He tastes good.

But I'm not a groupie.

My hands flat against his body, I push him away from me. "If that's how you avoid meaningful human interactions, then don't bother." I force my feet to move, and I go to the other side of the elevator and hit the button to make it move again, along with the button for the next floor. "You don't need to treat me like all the other girls. I get the point. I won't ask you any more questions."

The elevator opens, and I leave in a hurry. I don't turn back to look at him. *I can't.* And I don't check to see if he followed. *He didn't.*

* * *

Miles

I don't know what the hell that was about. Did she not come after me? Did she not send all the signals that said, "I'm not here for work, I'm here for play."? And I'm all about playing.

Then again, she's right. She was there last night. She saw what happened. And I *am* pissed as hell that Devon had the balls to come back to our suite and fuck Kennedy. This is what? The hundredth time they've made up? What's the point of sticking by a person who clearly doesn't give a shit about you? But Kennedy doesn't care. She sees that pretty boy with all his daddy's money and thinks the promise of fame is more important than love. And here I am, cleaning up more of her mess.

I leave the hotel and spot the orange Lamborghini ahead of me. It's no easy feat reaching it though. The paps swarm the valet loop, trying to get as close as possible to the Lambo. Then they spot me, and I'm screwed.

"Miles Riot!"

"Tell us what's going on with Tempest Ultra!"

"Who's the mystery woman touring with you?"

"Is she your girlfriend?"

I push my way through without speaking a word. Fuck these sorry excuses for reporters. They're nuisances. I reach the Lambo and pull open the passenger side door, getting in without an invitation. Shutting the door behind me mutes the noise outside, but the camera flashes are an annoying as hell distraction.

"Kaidan Stone," I say to the guy in the driver's seat. "I thought they had you locked up in that law office of yours."

"This is my office today," he says. Another pretty boy with all his daddy's money... He shifts the car into gear, and hits the gas, sending the paparazzi scattering.

I look over at Devon's twin brother. I'm not interested in games right now. "Can you tell me why you drove all the way out here? I'm pretty sure a phone call would've done just fine."

"Any excuse to hit Vegas, right?"

I don't buy that for one second, and Kaidan knows it.

He glances over at me as he shifts gears and weaves around traffic. "We want Tempest to sign to Stone."

I already knew that. "I still don't think it's a good idea." Not with the massive conflict of interest happening between Devon and Kennedy. One of their break ups could ruin all of our careers.

"I know you don't, but we're ready to prove it to you."

"You've already bribed us with the fancy bus and Vegas suite." And it's not enough to sway me. The Stones are the ones who have money to gamble. Tempest doesn't. "We don't need your gifts. We'll sign with the label who offers us a long-term career, and to be honest, signing with Stone isn't much of a guarantee. I'm pretty sure you know what I'm talking about." Devon and Kennedy's personal life hits the tabloids on a regular basis. Their unstable, dysfunctional fling is no secret.

"According to the tabloids, I'm pretty sure you're the one who went after my brother last night, not the other way around."

I set my jaw firm. Damn right I went after him. What's Kaidan going to do about it? "If he wants to start shit, I'm going to finish it. He needs to leave Kennedy alone, *especially* if you want us to sign."

Kaidan laughs. "Relax, man. I've had my share of fights with Devon. He's an asshole. No need to get defensive. It's obvious you prioritize the band's image, which is good, because the Stones prioritize the Stone image, and Devon is a loose cannon. How about a deal?"

He speeds through a yellow light and makes a right at the next intersection. This meeting'll last however long it takes to get back around to the hotel, and I'm not a fan of making spur of the moment decisions.

"We've got a month left on our shitty indie label. How about we get through our tour and talk after? Stone and Rev and whoever else wants us can keep fighting amongst themselves."

Kaidan remains as smooth and composed as ever. There's no guessing with him whether he's on your side or plotting your demise. No wonder he's working in entertainment law.

"It's not that easy, Miles. The other labels are watching, close. Assaulting paparazzi. Fighting in public. Causing scenes... Keep it up and next month, you'll be back to playing in your garage. No one will bother signing you." He reaches into the jacket of his suit and pulls out an envelope, handing it to me without looking away from the road. "Stay out of trouble. That goes for you, Kennedy, the rest of the band. And Devon."

"What?" What's that douchebag got to do with anything?

"Like I said, the Stone image is important, and Devon's a loose cannon. I don't give a shit what he's doing with your sister and neither should you. I *do* care what he's doing in public. So take that," he glances at the envelope, "as a reminder of what your life will look like if you play your cards right. Keep your band out of trouble, stay away from negative media attention, and get ahold of me at the first sign of Devon causing us more problems."

Stay away from media attention... Is now a good time to mention Abby? I open the envelope and pull out a check. Kaidan's own personal signature sits at the bottom. Three-hundred-thousand dollars. Fuck me.

"So another bribe? And if we don't end up signing to Stone?"

"Then you can fuck yourself." He pulls back up to the hotel and hits the brakes. "Sign to whoever the fuck you want. The money's not a bribe this time." He plasters on his big cocky grin. "Consider this a side gig. A contract job. Under the table."

I stuff the check back in the envelope, fold it, and shove it into my pocket. Without responding, I get out of his car and slam the door behind me. You've got to be fucking kidding me. I've spent years doing damage control for my own band. Now I'm on clean-up duty for the Stone family too? He wants me to stop fighting with Devon? Fine, the douchebag can be my new best friend for all I care. The last thing I need is to be on the Stones' bad side. Screwing up with them is like disappointing a drug cartel. If I fuck this up, my life is over.

* * *

Abby

My emergency elevator escape left me on a quiet floor, and I spent a good ten minutes pacing up and down the hallway before calling the elevator again to take me back up to the suite. He kissed me. *Miles Riot* kissed me. Why?! Was he trying to get me to shut up? Did he think that was the appropriate opportunity to make his move? Does he simply fuck every woman he comes in contact with?

I'm relieved to find the suite Miles-less when I return. I'm ready to punch him...or

pounce on him. That asshole. I'm here to
work, not have my head played with by some
hot rock star.

What's that smell?

I stop short of my room, where I'd had the
intention of hiding out until the bus left. Only, I can't help but notice how hazy the suite
looks. Devon and Nate sit on a couch passing
a bong back and forth, while Dax lounges in a
reclining chair. Great, they're getting high. I
can't stay here. I'll take my computer and find
a coffee shop or something.

Kennedy comes out of her room dressed
and chipper. "Hey roomie," she says to me,
which catches me off guard that much more.
"I'm leaving to get my hair done. You should
come with me."

Me? Is she talking to me?

"Aren't we leaving for Tucson soon?"

"We have plenty of time, and you can't
spend every minute working this week, right?
Come on."

If it gets me out of this reeking hotel room... "Sure," I agree with apprehension. I grab my purse and follow Kennedy out of the suite. We're halfway to the elevator when it opens. Miles steps off. My heart stops, and I try to ignore him. For a moment, he locks his gaze on me, and it's like I'm hypnotized. I can't look away. He smirks and continues toward the room, not stopping to talk to us. I need to know what he's thinking. I need to know why he kissed me. I still have to live with him for five and a half more days. I can't let it get awkward.

"You all right?" Kennedy asks me.

"Of course," I insist. "Everything's great... Perfect."

In the elevator, all I can do is relive moments ago when Miles had me pushed against the same wall Kennedy now stands next to. It makes for an awkward half minute while we wait to reach the lobby floor.

"So, blue or purple?" Kennedy asks me.

"Huh?" I'm still confused why she invited me.

"My hair. It needs a new color. What should I go with?"

Blue or purple? All right, that can be fun. "Um...purple?" I suggest as we start down the sidewalk outside. While I could never go that bold with my own hair, I have no problem living vicariously through the gutsy makeover choices of another woman.

"You know? Devon likes blue. I think I'll go with that."

Because we should always do whatever the man would like most... But I'm not about to get catty with her. I have to wonder though. If she dyes her hair the color she thinks Devon will like, what'll happen if—when?—they break up again? Will she have one of those celebrity breakdown moments where she shaves her whole head? That'll keep the tabloids happy.

Speaking of...

I barely notice the first camera click, but Kennedy looks over her shoulder, and when I check, I see not two this time, but three pap ratz with their cameras focused on us. No, focused on Kennedy. Fortunately, staying away from the spotlight means I'm on nobody's radar, and I'd like to keep it that way.

My pulse quickens and I feel a knot form in my throat. Last time these guys found Kennedy, a fight broke out. Now she doesn't have her bandmate to play bodyguard, but I can't imagine her *not* causing a scene.

Kennedy sighs and looks back at me. "How fast can you run?"

Me? I nearly failed my grade school fitness classes. "Is that necessary?"

She thinks for a second and shakes her head. "Nah." Behind us, one of the men call out to Kennedy. She spins around. "Hi boys," she says in a seductive tone while raising both her hands and holding up her middle fingers. The camera clicks keep pace with our steps as she turns around. "Almost there," she tells me. "Think I should flash them?"

"It'll be front page tabloid fodder by the morning if you do."

She contemplates it. "Ah. Fuck them. I'm in too good of a mood to care."

We get to the salon, and she turns around one more time, blowing them a kiss. "Bye boys."

I'm not sure which is worse, the Kennedy who lashes out at the paps or the one who teases them. Either way, she's only going to get more of them following her around.

Inside the salon, I breathe a sigh of relief. I hadn't considered the consequences of going out in public with Kennedy. And it wasn't until this moment that I realize how badly things could've gone. But surviving that mild close call is sort of exhilarating. Look at me, handling this assignment just fine. *In your face, Jonathan.*

"So how about you?" Kennedy says. We're standing at the reception desk, and I've got Kennedy and a stylist staring me down.

"Oh, I'm fine. I'll wait for you," I say.

"No you won't. We're getting our hair done, so make a fucking decision."

Well, okay then.

"I guess I can use a trim and maybe some highlights," I suggest.

"You're on tour with a rock band. Let me help you fit in better, country girl."

This cannot turn out well, but I can handle it. "Then what do you suggest, your majesty?"

She tilts her head back and laughs. "Yes! Some spunk. I like it. Trust me. You're already cute. I can make you hot."

Is that a compliment or a criticism? Not sure, but what the hell. "Fine. You call the shots."

We're led back to our chairs, and I stare at the mirror as Kennedy tells the stylist what to do with me. Thanks to the adrenaline rush of waiting for Kennedy to blow a fuse outside,

I'm still a little high off excitement. Plus, I could use a change. I've had the same natural-looking blond hairstyle for years. Something new would be fun...I might like it. *Miles might like it.*

Dammit. This is not about him.

"You ready?" the stylist asks me.

"Absolutely."

*

An hour later, we're back outside heading toward a coffee shop. Kennedy's new, periwinkle blue hair twists in big curls that hang to her mid back. It really is beautiful, but I'm distracted by my own new style. Don't get me wrong, I don't hate it, but I'm not sure it's me.

When I walked into that salon, my blond hair was long, wavy, light, and...normal. Now, it's six inches shorter, straightened, and bold enough to make me look far more edgier than I am. The blond is still there, but it transitions to a deep crimson about two-thirds of the way down. And some of the layers underneath are dyed a pitch black that mixes with the red making it darker, bolder, and a little sexy.

"You know what I did, right?" Kennedy asks as we're standing in line to order a couple lattes.

"What's that?"

"I let you stay true to yourself," she touches my blond hair before dropping her hand down to shake a fistful of my new gothic hair color, "while letting everyone know you have another side to you. A bad girl side. One who's not afraid to be naughty." She admires my hair for a few more seconds. "Like a sex goddess. I've created a masterpiece."

I laugh. "I think you're describing someone else." Bad girl? Naughty? Sex goddess? No way.

"Nope. I see it. Hell, I can already tell you have a thing for my brother, so you're definitely hiding something."

I feel my cheeks burn as she speaks and distract myself by placing my coffee order and waiting off to the side browsing the selection of mugs and coffee beans for sale.

"So it's true?" Kennedy comes up behind me. "You want Miles."

I turn toward her. "No. I don't even know him."

She doesn't look convinced. Our names are called and we take our drinks and leave, heading back to the hotel.

"I get it. Lots of women want my brother. But, friend-to-friend, I just want to make one thing clear..." She lets silence build the suspense, while I count the seconds before we're back at the suite. I don't want to be a part of this conversation. My own internal battle? I can deal with that. But other people knowing what I've been thinking, what I've been feeling...it makes it all too real.

Kennedy finally finishes her thought. "My brother is into a certain type of woman, and he's been on this nonstop hunt for 'the one' ever since he hit puberty. Problem is, when he think he's in love, it fucks him all up. He's not as good on stage, he stops working as hard, and he just, you know, loses sense of his priorities." We get to the casino and head toward the elevators. "I can't have him getting distracted, especially when I know which of these women aren't right for him." She punches the button to take us back up to our floor. "And sorry to say, but you're not."

"Why are you telling me all this? I already told you I'm not interested." And, if even entertaining the thought is this much of an issue, then I feel like I dodged a bullet pushing him away earlier.

"Good," she says in a cheery voice that I'm starting to learn is fake and manipulative. "Then you'll have no problem staying away from him. No more hanging out with him, chasing after him when he leaves, staring at him..."

The elevator doors open, and I'm the first one out. *This*. This is the real reason she

asked me to hang out. She needed me alone—
she needed to reel me in with her phony
kindness—so she could get control of me.
Well, like I said, I'm not interested in Miles,
so she wasted her time.

"Hey," she calls from behind me and I stop
short of the suite's door. "You understand
why I needed you to know all that? Everything's cool, right?"

I twist my face into the same fake expression she's got. Maybe my spunky new hairdo
really will bring out the bolder side of me after all. With a big smile, eyes wide, I say, "Oh
yeah. Everything's great!"

Kennedy looks pleased with herself. Mission accomplished, she must be thinking.
"Great. It's really nothing personal. It's just
best for you to remember why you're here and
keep to your work like the professional you
are."

"Of course. That's all I'm worried about,
and the faster I write, the faster I'll be able to
head back home."

"Good." Her false enthusiasm is starting to waver. "I'm glad we're friends now."

What? Are we battling to see who can out-bullshit the other?

"Me too." Hell, I even throw in a hug.

Chapter Six

Miles

I've got more money in my pocket than I've had in the last ten years combined. Devon Stone is high as a kite with my drummer and bass player, and we're scheduled to leave within the hour. With any hope, I just made a shit ton of extra cash to play babysitter for another ten minutes. Devon can go back to L.A. and wait for Kennedy there, and we can continue this tour in peace.

"Miles. You motherfucker. Get over here and take a hit. You seem tense," Dax says to me.

"I'm good. We should get ready to go." I hear the door open behind me and assume Ken's here now. Let's pack and get the hell out of Vegas.

The guys laugh. Nate stands up and walks over, patting my shoulder. "Okay, mom. We'll get right on that." I watch as he walks past and see it's not just Kennedy who came in. Abby's with her, and Nate makes another move. "Look at you, gorgeous." He walks up close to Abby and touches the side of her face. Her hair's different, in a good way. She looks even hotter than before. "When are you going to show up naked in my bed?" Nate asks her in his usual classy fashion.

Abby shakes her head. "When your pickup lines improve."

I can't help but smile at that shutdown, but then I remember this is the same woman who rejected me too. What do I care? Once we get to Tucson tonight, it'll take all of five minutes for me to find a woman to fuck. And that's all I'm worried about.

Lies.

I know it's not true. The easy lay is meaningless, and it's getting more mundane by the day. But why Abby? I hardly know her, and she's the last person who needs to be let into my private life. Anything she learns will probably end up in some magazine anyway.

But. I don't know. I want to know her. It's as unexplainable as that. It's something I want, and I don't like not getting my way.

A pounding on the door snaps me out of my thoughts. Eddie waltzes in. "Okay assholes. You're already late. Good thing the show's tomorrow night, huh, or we'd never get there in time. Now I want your asses on the bus in five. Got it?"

We're promised great food and entertainment tonight from Rev Records, courtesy of the private rooftop at some fancy place called

Chateau Monroe and the VIP lounge at Seductions Gentlemen's Club. Clearly, Rev isn't nearly as concerned with public image as Stone. It'll be an eventful night, so we take advantage of the six-hour drive to rest up. Devon and Kennedy are following in Devon's dumbass antique Camaro—I couldn't get rid of him as easily as I thought. Nate and Dax lounge on the couch with a few beers, and Abby sits to the side on her trusty laptop, the busy bee she is. I'm tempted to just go in the back room and pass out to avoid whatever the fuck's happening with my brain, but I'm Miles Fucking Riot, and if I want to hook up with a reporter, no matter how bad of an idea that is, I'll do whatever the hell I want.

"You finish your big story, yet?" I ask her, sitting down in the seat next to her.

At first, I don't think she's heard me. She doesn't look up. Doesn't respond. But then she says, "If the big story is a blank document, then I'm an overachiever."

"With everything you've seen already, you don't know what to write?"

Finally, she looks up at me and I take in her soft, blue eyes. "Paparazzi and drunken fights are hardly article-worthy."

That's a relief. "Most entertainment journalists would take whatever sells and run with it."

"I'm not like most journalists."

"I like the new hair," I say, suddenly changing the subject. "It seems to suit you more."

She considers the compliment for a second and clears her throat. "Thanks. Yeah, it's all right. Kennedy suggested it." When she says Ken's name, a different look passes across her face, like she's remembering something. "Anyway, I have to work, so..."

She focuses back on her computer, rejecting me for the second time today. Maybe she's mad I made a move on her. Oh well, most women would pay to make out with me. She should consider herself lucky. "Can't make that blank page any blanker," I say, getting up and walking away. I slam the bedroom door shut behind me and collapse onto the bed.

I lost track of the number of groupies I've fucked, but I can tell you one thing for sure. Love...that's a whole different ballgame and two lucky ladies have had that honor.

The first was Kara in third grade. Yeah, yeah. What little kid knows anything about love? It's not that though. Kara was an epiphany for my stupid, young brain. Her curly red hair and frilly dresses, she's the one who made me realize girls weren't just giggling annoying humans who didn't like dirt as much as I did. I spent weeks trying to get her attention before her family moved away. All right, so maybe that one wasn't love, but it sure as hell was heartbreak.

The other one was...

You know? I don't want to talk about it. Never mind her.

I reach over and grab my guitar by the neck, pulling it onto my chest. This girl, this sexy Ibanez ARZ, with its solid mahogany body and custom flat black paint job, is true love. I dig a guitar pick from my pocket and let my hands do what comes naturally. My fingers flick over the frets in a rushed dance that sounds like a sick solo. Maybe my mood calls for a new song.

I sit up and continue playing. Tempest is known for its quick-paced, raw feel that keeps the crowd moving. We're like one big 'fuck you' at the tune of dropped D. Kennedy may be the voice that leads us, but I do most of the songwriting. I started before her, but when I was running out of options and accepted that little sis had some potential, we teamed up. Still not sure that was the best idea with all the drama that came with working with her, but it's too late now.

Lyrics start running through my head as my hands continue to move without me thinking.

"To taste her skin
It's worth repeating.
To touch her lips—"

Wait. That's not shit Ken can sing. What the hell?

I try to refocus, but now the words are stuck with me. They keep rearranging themselves and I find my fingers slowing on the guitar. This is sounding less and less like a rock song and more and more like a—

Shit.

I drop the pick, tempted to drop the guitar too.

Quietly, I keep strumming the tune that's imbedded itself into my brain. Maybe if I entertain the thought, it'll pass without effect and I can move along to something worthy of a new single.

"She leaves me breathless
Mind a blur"

As I sing, a clear image forms in my mind. The curve of her hips. The sweetness of her smile. The taste of that rejected kiss on the elevator. Abby.

Knock, knock on the door, and my attention jolts in that direction. I doubt the band heard me playing this unwelcome tune, but I still feel like I've been caught in some embarrassing act, like I was in here jacking off or something.

"What's up?" I call out, acting cool.

The door opens, and Nate pops his head in. "Almost there. Get your ass out here and socialize."

"Bullshit. Tucson's hours away. I'm working in here."

He scrunches his forehead, looking confused. "You getting stoned too? You've been in here all afternoon." He shakes his head like I'm as oblivious as Dax on downers and leaves without another word.

Nate's got to be fucking with me. I find my phone and check the time. Holy shit. I've been working on this nonsense song for over three hours. That's impossible.

Or reporter chick's got me screwed up worse than any drug.

*

We have the entire rooftop to ourselves at Chateau Monroe, and our group, which grew after we picked up a few hot groupies, takes up one long table. I sit at one end with a blond girl in a green dress to my right and Eddie to my left. Next to Eddie is, Xavier, the vice president of Rev Records. He's schmoozing us tonight with bottomless glasses of fifty year aged red wine and anything we want on his tab. Fortunately, Devon sat this one out since it's enemy territory for Stone Records, but Nate, Dax, Kennedy, and a few nameless women are immersed in their own conversations down the table, and across from me, at the other end, seeming miles away, is Abby, who appears to be avoiding my eye contact. But why'd she sit directly in my view if she didn't want me to see her? And why would she wear that sexy cream-colored dress that hangs off her shoulders if she didn't want me to look at her?

Fucking mixed signals. And her song still plays in my head. *Her song?* It could be any woman's. Just because it's slower and more her style doesn't mean it's *hers*.

Oh, Miles. Always making excuses to mask your feelings.

Nate leans closer to Abby and says something I can't hear. She laughs, her smile gleaming, and I want to punch Nate. Instead, I finish off the glass of wine in front of me and ask the server to replace it with a double bourbon.

"So Miles," the woman next to me says, her eyelashes fluttering, "I can't wait for your show tomorrow night. I'll be in the front row." She winks, and I smile at the comical thought of this pretty girl being front and center in a rock crowd.

"Thanks. It'll be a good show." I'm throwing my typical professional lines at her, not really in the mood to flirt. Though...I am in the mood to fuck.

I glance down at Abby again and catch her watching me. I hold her gaze until she breaks it, an involuntary smile starting to form on her face. She returns to her conversation with Nate and acts like she's completely engaged in whatever he's telling her. I make a mental note to myself. Nate's trying to seal the deal with her before me. If that's how it'll be, consider the race on, buddy.

The food starts to arrive—plates of fresh bread, escargot, calamari, some sort of crab dip. I keep an eye at the other end of the table as we all dig in.

"Not bad, eh Miles?" Xavier asks me. For a second, I think he's referring to Abby, but I snap out of it. Pathetic, man. I'm acting fucking pathetic.

"Is this a Rev Records promise every night if we sign?"

Xavier and Eddie both laugh.

"If that's what you want," Xavier says. "But more importantly, you'll have an EP out by Winter, an international tour next year, and all the publicity you can imagine. You'll be the biggest rock act in the world after we get ahold of you."

Oh, the promises. So many of them, yet they all say the same thing. It won't matter who we sign with at this point. The interested labels are all the frontrunners of the industry, which is why we're letting them fight for us. The perks have been excessive and extreme—money, luxury, privileges. We could get used to this. But we all know what's coming. Once we sign, the label will own us. We won't have nearly the power we have now, so we're enjoying the freedom at their expense for as long as possible.

More food arrives. This time, enormous plates with microscopic portions of fancy food. What the hell is this shit? How about a cheeseburger? They could use some of that truffle mushroom stuff if they want to hike up the price, but we're a rock band, not professional food critics with discriminating palettes.

But it's not the food that annoys me. It's Nate. And how he has Abby laughing. She's all relaxed with him, yet she was all cold with me? What did I do? Besides kiss her. And don't tell me she isn't interested. The way her mouth begged for me. The way her body moved into me. She wanted more. But she stopped.

So why's she giving Nate the time of day?

Dax and one of the nameless groupies get up to excuse themselves. The woman claims she needs to use the restroom, and I smirk. I'll be surprised if they show back up. Our hotel's right across the street—a swanky place with a top floor suite waiting for us. They're off to fuck, and suddenly the seat next to Abby, across from Nate, is empty and calling for me.

The blond next to me watches with disappointment as I get up and walk away from her. Sorry, honey. I've got other goals.

"How's it going down here?" I ask, dropping into the empty seat. I grab Dax's half empty glass of wine and drain it. Glancing over at Abby, she's still smiling, but I see it. A wall she instantly puts up in my presence. Nate looks over at me, clearly annoyed.

"Not bad. How's your *date*?" he asks me, looking down at the other end of the table. The woman who'd been vying for my attention is now flirting with Eddie. Nice work, man.

"Think she's more your type." I turn to Abby. "You going out with us after this?"

She looks at me and her eyes say so much. There's a want, a need, in them. But she breaks eye contact looking past me. I follow her gaze to Kennedy.

"I'm gonna need a pizza after this," Kennedy says, laughing as she cleans her plate. She's staring in our direction and in a surprisingly decent mood considering her boyfriend isn't with her. "I'm all for this glamorous amuse-bouche type shit, but I want fifty more plates of it. Do you know what this was, Abby?"

Abby clears her throat. "Um, I think the server said it was confit de canard."

"Ah. Okay. See? We don't know this stuff. We're more onion rings and milkshakes type people. But I knew I could count on you. This seems more your style, right?"

Abby raises an eyebrow. "I wouldn't say that, but—"

"Definitely more your type than ours," Kennedy insists. I don't know what she's getting at. She's probably drunk. "It's like we live in completely different worlds."

Kennedy laughs again and this time Abby joins her, but I can tell it's forced.

"Right," she says. "Way different worlds."

"Speaking of different worlds," Nate says to Abby, "it's a proven fact opposites attract."

"You think so?" Abby asks him. Now she sounds more amused and genuine.

"I do, which is why I think you should let me take you out sometime."

Abby shakes her head smiling. "And what about the two girls next to you?" she asks, lowering her voice.

The two women to Nate's right are whispering to each other while they eat. Every now and then they look over at Nate and giggle. One of them has dyed pitch-black hair and a nose ring. The other is in a corset dress and lacy gloves. A couple goth girls, they're exactly the type Nate likes to take home with him.

"There's plenty of me to share, Abby." He stretches his arm around one of the women, pulling her closer to him. "All three of you can have me at once, if you prefer."

"I'm down with that," the woman says. Her friend perks up with excitement.

I check Abby's reaction. Eyes wide, mouth slightly open. I can't tell if she's mortified or horrified. But either way, I'm satisfied.

"No thanks." Abby reaches for her wine glass but notices it's empty.

I flag the server and have him refill it.

"Thanks," she says, smiling at me as she drinks half the glass. Her expression tells me everything as she subtly shakes her head and looks at me with an expression that screams, *Is Nate serious?!*

I laugh. "Nate's quite the ladies man. Not sure you'd want to pass that up."

She rolls her eyes, while Nate pretends to be offended.

"That's fine," he tells Abby. "Keep rejecting me. You're the one who'll be missing out."

"And I'm sure I'll regret it 'til my last breath."

*

After dinner, we leave Chateau Monroe and head east toward the strip club. After the wine and liquor, we're all a little unstable on our feet. Nate's relying on his two goth girls to keep him upright. Dax and his friend have graced us with their presence after "going to the restroom" for forty-five minutes, and

Kennedy skips along beside them. Eddie and Xavier split to go talk contracts, and I don't know what happened to the girl who was trying to hook up with me. Abby follows behind the group, and I slow my pace to match hers.

"Ever been to a strip club?"

"I have not," Abby says with hesitation. "And I'm not sure tonight's a good night for firsts."

"It's not what you think. You'll have fun." From the corner of my eye, I watch her as she walks.

Her dress lies loose over her body and every move by her looks graceful and sexy. Her hips sway, her spunky new hair dances behind her. If I had my way, I'd press her up against any one of these buildings and kiss her, touch her. God damn, I want to touch her. I subtly step closer so my arm grazes hers. The second we touch, I see her inhale quickly. She wants it too. I'm not just being cocky. I can sense it. So why close me off? Why not just go for it?

Maybe Seductions Gentlemen's Club will loosen her up.

Abby crosses her arms in front of her like she's cold. "Yeah, I don't know about fun, but, I mean, I'm sort of obligated to follow along, right? The job and all. My boss wants me fully immersed in your life—I mean, in the rock star life."

I'd like her fully immersed in *my* life, I want to tell her. But the wrong thing will scare her off. She already seems seconds away from fleeing.

"How about we come up with a signal?"

She eyes me suspiciously.

I continue, "No, really. I'll help you escape if you hate it. We can use a code word or hand wave or—"

"A hand wave?" She laughs, and I'm relieved to hear her relax with me, even if for only a second.

"All right fine. That might be too obvious. We'll stick with the code word." I'm saying whatever comes to mind. As long as I keep talking, she'll keep listening and she's much too polite to interrupt me and leave. It's ingrained in her sweet, Southern upbringing. "Country girl," I say.

"Oh, because that's not bizarre to shout out at a strip club."

"No need to shout it. You can whisper it in my ear." As fast as I say it, I see her tense up again. "Or, you know, use it in a sentence. You're a writer. You can manage that."

We continue walking in silence for a moment before she responds again. "Fine. *Country girl*, it is. And then what? You'll come to my rescue? You think I need rescuing?"

There she goes again, proving to me she's strong and independent, as though I hadn't caught on. "I'll let you be the judge of that."

She quickens her pace and catches up to the others. Kennedy wraps an arm around her shoulders in a friendly gesture, and I enjoy my view of Abby from behind. It's a gorgeous view, I must say.

We're passing a music store with a huge window display, and it's got everything. Five thousand dollar drum kits, electric guitars and basses made with solid-body quilted maple, high end synthesizers and mixing equipment. But it's the instrument in the corner, propped high on a stand that pulls my attention from Abby's fine ass. Exotic black heart sassafras body, a sitka spruce front stained a deep blue, phosphor bronze strings. It's a breathtaking acoustic guitar and something I never in my life considered buying before. Not when I live off distortion pedals and DiMarzio Breed pickups. But this one calls to me, and while the $10,000 price tag would've scared me away in the past, I don't even flinch now. Thanks to Kaidan Stone, I've got money to burn.

And thanks to Abby Clarke, I've got a song to finish.

Chapter Seven

Abby

One second, Miles is right behind me, and another, he's gone. I try not to be obvious as I check over my shoulder, but Mr. Suave promised to be my emergency rescue if need be. He won't be much help if he's off in an ally making out with a groupie.

And what's that, my pounding heart? Is that disappointment? Jealousy? God, I hope I'm just drunk. I take a deep breath, trying to settle my nerves. Kennedy's arm around me is a good reminder of what I'm here for. Now I just need to stop focusing on a guy who wouldn't know how to have a real relationship if a professional love guru tattooed the instructions on his forehead.

"Here we are," Kennedy sings and I look up at the sign.

A curly "Seductions" in pink neon looks more like a warning sign than a welcome to me. If touring with a rock star is a different world, going to a strip club is a different universe.

Hope the drinks are strong.

We walk in and it's exactly what I expect. Everything is glowing in blues and purples and reds. The lights are dim and the music loud. On one end there's a bar with bartenders busy mixing and serving the crowds of patrons. On the other end of the building is a big stage where three women are currently selling their dignity.

Sorry. That's judgmental of me. I don't know them, nor do I know why they're in this career. Maybe they like it. I feel bad for my snap judgment, but I'm just as uncomfortable as I'd expected.

Country girl. Country girl.

Miles still isn't here.

The floor is filled with tables and lounge areas. I see at least two bachelorette parties and several groups of guys egging each other on to get closer to the stage, their fists filled with singles.

Other tables have solo patrons who clearly came for the show, and I swear I see at least one couple on a date. They're sitting side-by-side, comfortable as can be, smoking cigars as they get a private dance at their table. Consider my mind blown.

"Here," someone says to the right of me. It's Dax with a tall drink of something fruity-looking. "Looks like you need it."

I snatch it from him. "You have no idea."

"From the look on your face, I think I have a pretty good idea. Now come on."

I look around to see the group is being led through a beaded curtain to another room. Oh great, more surprises. I take one last look at the front door. Still no Miles. Well, screw him. This drink will be my knight in shining armor—this one and the one after. We're led down a short hallway where a half-naked woman holds a velvet curtain open for us.

"Welcome," she says, as if she's a flight attendant welcoming us onto a plane. "Enjoy your night."

Inside, we're greeted with plush couches making up three sides of a square around the room and a low, round stage in the middle. Little end tables sit between the sofas and a server is ready and waiting for our orders. The walls are covered in mirrors, and I can't help it. I use the old hotel trick to see if it's fake. The reflection of my fingertip smashes into my finger—no space left between—and I know that means there are people watching

on the other side. Makes sense though. Got to
keep the employees safe. Nate and his girls
take up the middle couch while Dax and his
friend plop down on the couch closest to the
door. I choose the spot furthest from everyone, hoping most of the action takes place
around the guys. As soon as I sit, I notice my
newest BFF Kennedy sits down next to me.

"You excited?" she asks me.

Not at all. I've never been more nervous
and uncomfortable. I'd take mosh pits and
crowd surfing any day compared to...this. "As
long as they keep these drinks coming, I'm
good. How are you?" I keep my voice perky
and phony, just like hers.

"I'm great. I wish Devon could be here.
But...you know...gorgeous men, naked girls.
It's better to keep him away." She winks.

The curtain moves to the side again, and I
hold my breath, worrying I'll give myself
away as Miles walks in. He's alone, so maybe
he didn't get side tracked by some woman. I
conceal my relief by focusing on my glass.

"Hey, thanks again for being understanding," Kennedy says, placing a hand on my leg. "You're a great reporter. I wouldn't want your job to be compromised."

I nod slowly. "Of course." Is she threatening me now? Or does she think the issue's been resolved?

Miles sits next to Dax, a low ball glass in his hand. He looks across at me as our entertainers saunter in. A chandelier hanging in the center of the room changes from a soft yellow to a more seductive pink glow, and music starts. Everyone but me reacts by clapping and hollering excitedly, and it takes me a second to realize they're not doing it for the scantily dressed women. The song that's playing through the overhead speakers is one of their singles. Kennedy's the most surprised and pleased as the room fills with her vocals.

Three women take to the little stage in the center of our VIP room. All eyes are on them as the server comes around behind us, placing fresh drinks on our tables. I quickly gulp down the rest of what was in my glass and grab for the new one. No way am I getting through this without being as drunk as possible.

At first, the girls are dancing together. I notice Nate, especially, loves this. They peel the clothes off their coworkers and get close enough to kiss. But as soon as they're down to the tiniest lingerie I've ever seen, they break away and move toward each of the couches. I try not to look horrified as I realize it's just me and Kennedy on this couch.

This is not good.

Our dancer has long, dark hair and dark skin. She's beautiful and I hope she took this job to pay for a law degree or something. She's wearing a silk babydoll dress that ends just below her hips and I can blatantly see she's wearing a black g-string underneath.

"Can we touch the dancers?" Kennedy asks seductively. I feel my cheeks burn. Kissing Miles in the elevator was risqué enough for me. This? This is miles away from my level of comfort.

"Tempest Ultra can do anything they want tonight," the dancer replies. "I'm Jasmine, by the way."

"You're very lovely, Jasmine. And I especially appreciate your choice of soundtrack tonight."

My attention wanders to the rest of the room as Kennedy enjoys the attention from her own private dancer. Jasmine must be professional enough to catch on to my resistance here. She gives me space, and I'm tempted to tip her just for that reason.

Nate seems to be in heaven on his couch where his dancer has removed her top and is shimmying her breasts right in his face. His female friends on either side of him are taking her direction as they smother Nate in kisses while rubbing their hands all over him.

I shake my head, trying to hold off judgment again. This is just their thing. It's okay that it's not *my thing*. But then I look across from me. The third dancer is in Miles's lap, her back pressed against his chest as she grinds against him. Suddenly, I feel sick.

My stomach twists as I watch her reach down and massage his legs with her hands inching closer and closer to his—

I break my concentration, looking away, but with mirrors on every wall, I can't find a single direction that's not displaying Miles and Miss Half Naked practically getting it on. Never mind that Miles is fully clothed or that he's keeping his hands to himself. Though I'm watching his reflection, he doesn't take notice. I see him grab his drink and finish it. He nearly drops the glass when he goes to put it down. Between the lack of coordination and his heavy eyelids, it's more than obvious he's wasted. His dancer bends herself in half, wiggling her butt in front of him. He's looking away though.

No, not just away. He's looking ahead of him. Toward me. I watch him watching me, and I want to scream, *what is going through your head?!* What is he thinking? Why does he act like a manwhore and then return his attention to me? This isn't something I could ever get used to, so it's no use. Maybe I need to spell it out for him.

Miles and I would never work. Kennedy's right.

The dancer spins around and straddles Miles. I feel acid creeping up my esophagus. I'm grossed out. Then she kisses him. Is that even part of the job description, lady? Her mouth stays on his and an image flashes across my mind of us in the elevator. Miles kissing me. He goes for anything with a vagina, doesn't he?

I think I'm going to be sick. Before they break away from each others' faces, I storm out of the room. This *country girl* doesn't need someone to rescue her. I can take care of myself. I leave the club and get outside, sucking in the fresh air. The sick feeling doesn't go away.

Dizzy and uncoordinated, I work my way back to the hotel, pulling out my phone as I walk. It's not too late to call Dee, is it?

"Abby? You okay?"

"I'm fine," I slur. "How are you? How's Chord?"

"We're fine and you sound drunk. Must be having fun."

"Not exactly," I say. "I'll pay you $5000 to come take my place. Please."

"Do you have $5000?"

"No." I hear her laugh at the other end of the line. The familiar sound cheers me up. "I'm thinking of strangling Jonathan when I get back. He knew this would be awful for me."

"What's wrong?" she asks, this time her voice filled with genuine worry.

But I'm not about to tell her about Miles or my confusing feelings toward him or Kennedy's masked threats to me.

I give the easy answer. "It's just a completely different world. One I don't belong in." I reach the hotel and give the concierge my name. Another minute passes and I have the key to our suite. I'm looking forward to hiding out in the privacy of my room for the night.

"That's bullshit," Dee tells me. "You may be out of your comfort zone, but you have to make the most of it. Look for the opportunity. When things like this happen in life, you treat it as a learning experience. Do something you've never done before. Take risks. Learn more about yourself. I think Jonathan knew what he was doing assigning this to you. The magazine's under a lot of pressure right now, and he has to know his staff is capable of doing anything, anytime, anywhere. To be honest, I think this is a test."

Wow. I didn't even consider that. I knew Lydian was looking to bring in fresh faces, which meant weeding out anyone who wasn't making the cut. Am I close to being fired? That would destroy everything, including my chances of landing another music journalist job. They'd all see me as unworthy.

"You still there?" Dee asks as I step into the elevator and use my key card to bring me up to the penthouse.

"Yeah. I'm here." I try to wrap my head around everything, but it's impossible with the amount of alcohol I let myself consume. I lean back against the wall of the elevator, hoping the phone will cut out before I have to talk more about this.

"You're limitless, Abby. You're a grown woman who has a world of potential ahead of her. Don't let any of this make you feel like an outsider, okay."

Okay... But the word doesn't come out of my mouth.

Dee continues, "Find what you want, girl. Go after it. Oh, and Chord says hi. He misses you."

I miss me too.

I assure Dee I'm fine and hang up. What's happening to me? My sights should be on my career before I blow it. Instead, I'm getting caught up in unwelcome feelings for Miles. Kennedy's calling the shots. I'm letting myself be the tagalong on this tour.

Enough.

I go into our suite and pick a room with a large king sized bed. It might be the only single room in this penthouse, but see if I care. I'm claiming it tonight.

I collapse on the bed, covering my face with my hands. Tonight, regroup. Recharge. Tomorrow, get back to work.

My phone rings again, and I'm sure it's just Dee double-checking that things really are okay.

"Hello?"

"Hi, Abigail Clarke?"

"Yes?" I sit up in bed and clear my throat. "Who's calling?"

"My name's Polly Hemsworth. I work with *ScandalLust*. I wanted to ask you a couple questions."

Is she serious? "I'm sorry. You work for a tabloid, and you're calling me why? How'd you get this number?"

She ignores my questions. "Is it true the band is involved in illegal drug activity?"

Like smoking pot? How's that newsworthy? And if they're doing more, why would I know about it? But I'm not giving them any reason at all to speculate. "Of course not," I tell her. I really should just hang up, but...

"And is it true, Miles is holding secret meetings with a drug cartel?"

I burst out laughing and fight to catch my breath. "I'm sorry," I say in the best professional tone I can muster. "I think you have your facts mixed up. Miles isn't some ringleader of a drug scheme."

There's a pause before Polly answers, "We have reason to believe he is, Ms. Clarke, and we plan on running the story as soon as possible. We just need your help."

"Why would I help you? I don't work for you."

"You don't," she says. "But you could. In fact, we're interested in paying for any information you dig up while you're on tour with the band. Any photos or secrets they're hiding...and we're certain they're hiding many."

"Well, I'm not interested in being paid to act unethical. I report what's on the record and I do so in a legitimate form of media. I *don't do* celebrity scandal trash."

"Fifty-thousand dollars, Ms. Clarke."

"Excuse me?"

"We'll pay you fifty-thousand dollars for any story you give us that can make the cover."

She's got to be out of her mind. Fifty thousand?

"Just think about it. We'll be in touch."

She hangs up before I can argue, not that I had anything planned to say. I'm still paralyzed by the fifty-thousand dollars. The things I could buy with that.

But for what sacrifice? To tell lies? Tempest Ultra aren't involved in some drug scheme. *ScandalLust* is grasping at straws, like usual. And I'm not going to play into their games.

*

I must have been long passed out by the time everyone got back to the penthouse. I didn't hear a sound, and this morning, it's just as quiet. Aside from an invasive headache, I'm thinking much clearer today. The wide open windows let in all the morning sunlight, and the incredibly comfortable chaise lounge in the living room offers a welcoming spot to finally start this article. I've decided it's simply going to be an opinion piece about breaking out of my own shell and experiencing life as a rock star. This'll keep Tempest Ultra in a positive light while giving readers something entertaining. My goal is they can live vicariously through my experiences. I know for a fact Jonathan will like it.

I'm barely a sentence in when I hear noise behind me.

"Can't you leave later?" I hear Kennedy ask. I peek over my shoulder to see Devon walking out with a small duffel bag.

"Sorry. Gotta get some work done before I head to London."

Kennedy gives him an exaggerated pout while wrapping her arms around his neck and digging her fingers into his hair. I feel like I'm eavesdropping, but I was out here first. It's not like I'm hiding.

"I'll fly you over as soon as you finish the tour, okay?" Devon tells her.

She gives a little squeal. "To London. That'll be amazing, baby. I can't wait."

Kennedy kisses him before Devon turns and heads toward the door. Another minute of listening to them express their goodbyes and then I hear Kennedy. "I love you," she tells her boyfriend.

The door closes behind him and I notice he never said, I love you too.

Kennedy prances over and plops down next to me. Great, she's going to do the best friend thing again. I give her an awkward smile and continue to work. Two sentences in and she interrupts me.

"So, whatcha writing?"

"I'm just working on this article." My eyes never leave my screen.

"Oh yeah?" She moves closer to me, her legs smashed against mine now. "Are you going to talk about me?"

I can't tell if she's concerned I might or hoping I will. "I'll be talking about the whole band...but it'll be good stuff. Don't worry." I don't need her telling me how to do my job next.

"Fun." She leans back against the couch, and a door opens to our right, revealing Dax and the same girl he was with last night. They stagger into the kitchen and start making enough noise to wake the rest of the penthouse.

"I'm going to go work," I tell no one in particular and get up to go back to my room. So much for the quiet concentration.

"Let me know if you want me to proofread it when you're finished," Kennedy says to me, her smile beaming.

"Sure will." I don't bother with the fake enthusiasm this time. Her hovering is getting to be annoying, and I don't need her intruding on any more of my life.

Behind the closed door of my room, I let out a sigh of relief. Only a couple more days, I tell myself. A couple more days with these people and I can be finished. I sit at the oak desk near the window and try to refocus on the story. I finish a paragraph before my computer dings, alerting me to a new message. I give in to procrastination and open it up.

From: P. Hemsworth
Subject: Offer's on the table
Message: *Hi Abby,*

It was so nice to hear from you last night. I enjoyed our chat. In regard to the topic we discussed, please know the monetary agreement still stands. One story. $50,000. Please respond once you're ready to move forward.

Thank you,

Polly

ScandalLust Magazine

I was hoping she'd given up, but I shouldn't be that naive to think the tabloids would let up on a story they want. I've seen them in action. They're relentless, weaseling their way to whatever information—true or false—that can make them money.

But the fifty-thousand dollars... It's tempting. I convince myself it's okay to give it some thought. Maybe there's a way I can take advantage of this, make it spin my way.

I resolve to entertain the idea later, after I've gotten the first draft of this article finished. As soon as I click to close out of my email, I hear the ping sound again. Is Polly going to be hounding me all day?

No. This isn't my email this time. It's my messenger application.

How does one book time with a driven, very busy journalist?

It's from Miles. I sit there staring at the screen, the cursor blinking in the reply box waiting for me. He's waiting for me. What am I supposed to say? After last night, he's proven to me he has no interest in anything more than a one-night stand, and that's not something I participate in.

I write back my usual response.

Me: *Sorry. I'm working.*

He'll get distracted and go after the next pair of legs he likes. And I'm completely, totally okay with that. Miles can live his life however he wants.

But then why do I feel like there's a rock in my throat? And why am I watching, unblinking, our chat box, to see the second he writes back?

Do I have feelings for him? More than just ordinary lust for an attractive rock star?

Not a chance. We don't know each other at all. It's just a distraction from my work. I'm a writer. I'll do anything to procrastinate.

Miles: *So then, should I schedule a meeting with your assistant?*

Me: *I don't have an assistant.*

Miles: *Are you hiring?*

I laugh.

Me: *Are you applying?*

Miles: *If it'll let me have a real conversation with you without you putting up walls and pushing me away.*

Ouch. Could he be any more abrupt? I start typing my response but delete everything I think to say.

I'm not—

I'm here to work. I can't—

I'm sorry—

I settle on being just as blunt as him.

Me: *What do you want from me?*

Miles: *Five minutes of your time.*

Me: *Now?*

Miles: *Tonight. After the show.*

Isn't that when he performs his ritual of picking out a groupie to take home? Does he think I'll take on that role that easily? I start to tell him no, but second-guess myself. I'm making up assumptions. He just wants to talk. It'll be fine.

Me: *Okay. Tonight.*

This article's never going to be finished with everything weighing on my mind now. *ScandalLust.* Miles.

When I get back home, I'm demanding a raise.

Chapter Eight

Abby

I'm lying if I say I didn't put extra thought into getting dressed tonight. It's just a rock show, sure, but I don't know what to expect after. I want Miles to know I'm not putting up with any crap from him. And I want him to see me exactly how I am. So I went with a plaid button-down opened up over a white tank top, and I paired it with a jean skirt and wedge heels. I may not fit in with the crowd, whose wardrobe consists of all the same shade of black, but it doesn't matter. I'm standing backstage anyway.

Tempest is on their encore, and my heart is pounding. We're down to the last minutes of this show, and then what? Then I find Miles.

The audience rocks back and forth along with the song. Kennedy belts her lines while Miles fills in with background vocals. I find myself focusing on his voice, and it sends chills down my spine. I could listen to him sing all night, and that fact terrifies me. *Stick to your guns, Abby.* This is one rock star who's in for a dose of reality when he learns I don't play games.

One of Dax's drumsticks snap in half and he replaces it without missing a beat. Impressive. The music only grows louder, an audience of heads are banging, and then a beer bottle comes flying overhead from the crowd and crashes into Dax's jaw. My hands snap to my own face in shock. My god. Is he all right?

He shakes it off as nonchalantly as though a fly were buzzing around his head, and he still doesn't miss a beat. Bloods seeps from a cut right next to his mouth. It's grotesque, yet he's unfazed. Forget the broken drumstick being impressive. This is downright insane.

Is it true the band is involved in illegal drug activity?

Polly's question comes back to me as I watch Dax play the song all bloodied up. I've seen them all getting high on pot, but is he involved in something stronger? Something that would make him oblivious to pain? Is *ScandalLust* on to something?

Or maybe it's just adrenaline. These are rock stars, after all. They can handle some pain and gore. I'm grasping at straws to think it's more than that.

The song comes to an end, and I'm thrown back into reality. It's time to meet with Miles.

I give them a few minutes to get backstage and unwind. In the bathroom, I stare at myself in the mirror, concentrating on my breathing. *Relax.* Think of it like any other interview. It's my job to talk to Miles. He might give me something to use in the article. So it's an obligation. No big deal.

I keep repeating this in my head as I turn to leave. The bathroom door opens, and Kennedy waltzes in. I don't give her a second to steal the upper hand here.

"Great show tonight!" A huge smile plastered on my face, I pat her on the back and walk out. If anyone can intimidate me and make me change my mind about meeting Miles, it's her.

I find Nate and Dax in the warm-up room, but Miles is nowhere to be found. Eddie and a woman walk in behind me. The woman, carrying a bag, walks up to Dax, reaches for his face, and tilts his head to get a better look at the cut. She's a nurse, I presume?

"Are you all right?" I ask Dax.

He shrugs his shoulders. "I'm fine. Eddie's being mama bird though. You're too protective, old man."

Eddie smirks. "Right. Next time you get injured, I'll let you bleed out, 'kay asshole? Now do as the nice nurse says and maybe she'll give you a lollipop."

Dax sits down on a stool as the nurse pulls out supplies. "Just a couple stitches," she says.

Gross. I don't want to stand around to watch. "You guys know where Miles is?"

Nate turns around, suddenly intrigued. "Why go running after Miles when I'm right here?"

"I'm charmed, really." This guy's hysterical to me. So much confidence bundled up inside him. It's so over-the-top, it's ridiculous. I don't know how anyone takes him seriously. "We have a meeting," I say, trying to sound professional.

"Mhmm." Nate nods and raises an eyebrow. "A *meeting*—"

"Try a couple doors down on the left," Dax says and is just as quickly told not to move his mouth. "I better get my lollipop after this."

"Thanks," I mutter and walk out of the room.

The hallway is lit up in bright fluorescents and the doors are all painted different colors. The first on the left is green. The second red. I stop in front of the red one, not missing the symbolism here. Red—danger, stop, caution.

I reach for the knob but stop when I hear noise from inside. Someone's in here, that's for sure. But what if it's not Miles? What if I'm about to interrupt someone else? I take a step back and check the next door on the left. It's further down and blue. He could be down there. I consider walking away, but then I hear his voice.

He's definitely in this red room.

And he's...singing.

"Quiet contemplation
Blaring recognition"

I push the door open slowly, and when I spot him inside, my heart stops.

"Soul's evaluation

Screaming desperation"

I get inside and close the door, looking around. It's just another warm-up room, a smaller one. There's a wall with a big counter and mirror. There's a couch. And there's Miles, sitting on a stool in the middle of the floor, holding an unbelievably beautiful acoustic guitar. I recognize it as one of my top dream guitars if I had the money. And it sounds just as amazing as I expected.

But hold the phone. Miles is playing it. Miles is singing along with it. And it's definitely not a Tempest song.

"She leaves me breathless

Mind a blur

Fate's dirty tricks

Now I want her"

I gulp. What is this? He—he wrote me a song? And not just a song. He's written dozens of rock songs ranging from a fast punk sound to the double bass of metal. This is nothing like anything he's written before.

This is just for me.

It's slow. Sensual. Sweet. Quiet.

Just my style.

I smile at him and shake my head. "What are you doing?" I ask quietly, but I hope he doesn't stop playing. I want to keep listening. My nerves are on fire, and I don't know whether I want to cry or jump on him. This is a side of Miles I never expected. And it's a side of him I definitely want to know. My chest heaves as I try to calm my breathing, but I'm overwhelmed and amazed and...turned on.

"To taste her skin
This can't be fleeting"

Dee told me to take risks. Kennedy tried telling me we'd never work. My mind's been tuned in on Miles for days. If there's any time to take a chance, this is it.

"To touch her lips
It's worth repeating"

I reach behind me and twist the lock on the door. It's now or never. I move toward Miles.

"She leaves me breathless—"

I steal his lyrics with a kiss, my mouth pressing to his. His lips are warm, smooth, just like on the elevator, but the feelings between us are heightened. We both want this, whether it's right or wrong. Whether we can work or not.

His tongue plunges into my mouth dancing with my own, and I love the way he tastes. I hear the guitar drop to the floor, and Miles's hands grip my hips, pulling me closer to him. He wraps his hands around my back, and I feel his strength as he tries to close the space between us. But we're already as close as we can get. It's not good enough. I want him on me. In me.

I climb onto his lap, straddling him, and he lifts me up, effortlessly, moving us to the countertop under the huge, lit-up mirror. He pushes my shirt away from my shoulders, and I can't hold in the moan that escapes me as he kisses and nibbles at the skin on my shoulder, my neck. He kisses my jaw and moves back in toward my mouth. I savor the feel of him, the taste of him, as he kisses me with every ounce of the pent up energy we've kept contained.

His fingers weave their way into my hair and tug. I cry out in ecstasy, and fumble to get Miles out of his tight black shirt. I throw it to the floor and take in his taut, tattooed chest. I trail my hands over his skin and give a shudder of a breath. I look back up to see him watching me intently. I move his messy hair away from his face and he turns to my palm, kissing it.

This feels too good to be true. I'm living someone else's life right now.

"I don't want to be your one-night stand."

I don't know where that came from or whether or not I instantly regret it. If that was his intent, then this moment is over before it began. But I hold my head up firmly committed to my words.

"There are hundreds of women out there who would."

Is he challenging me? "So that's all you think this is?"

I'm ready to get up and leave, feeling suddenly empty and let down. But then Miles's smile gives him away and he leans in to kiss me again. "No. It's not," he says. He lifts me off the countertop and carries me to the plush couch on the other side of the room, laying me down gently.

"Then what's going on with us?" I ask him.

He pulls my plaid shirt off, dropping it to the floor and kneels down next to me. His fingers rake the bottom hem of my tank top and slowly push it up my stomach. He leans down and kisses my bare skin. My back arches, not wanting his mouth to leave my body.

He looks back up at me and touches the side of my face. His thumb slides down my cheek, over to my mouth, where he brushes across my bottom lip. "I don't know," he finally answers. "But I want to find out." He stands up, tall above me now. I feel vulnerable and ready to give in to anything he wants. "Do you want to find out too?"

No words come to me, but I nod. Yes, please. Whatever this could lead to, I want it. And I want it now.

He goes to the end of the couch and carefully takes off my heels. Wherever his hands touch, his lips follow as he runs his hands up my ankles, my shins, my thighs. He reaches the bottom of my skirt and instead of taking it off, he reaches underneath and takes my panties off with an urgency. Lustful energy floods the room as his hands explore under my skirt. His fingers discover their new territory with a gentleness that leaves my body aching. I feel the pressure building as he runs a finger up and down the folds of my sex. There's no hiding the heat, the wetness. He knows how much I want him. I press my leg against his inner thigh and confirm he wants me just as much. I reach down and unbutton my skirt. Kicking it off me and giving him a front row view of me. Instead of gawking, he leans down, kissing and massaging my clit. I let out a moan and grip at his back, my nails digging into his shoulders. He looks up at me, smiling, and continues his journey of kisses up my hips, my belly, slowly pushing my shirt higher and higher until he yanks it off over my head and crushes his mouth into mine again.

I reach down and find the button of his jeans. I yank down the zipper and push the denim down, urging him to help me out. There's far too much fabric between us. He stands up and removes his pants and boxer briefs. My breath catches as I scan him from head to toe. He's gorgeous with clothes on. He's intoxicating without them. Miles reaches behind me and unclasps my bra with one hand.

This is it. Two bodies naked and wanting. Whatever happens after, at least I know right now, I'm doing exactly what I want. Miles leans down and pulls a foil packet from his jeans pocket. I'm reminded again how often he does this, and the look on my face must give away my thoughts.

"Don't worry. I didn't have alternative plans tonight. I just had high hopes the song would work."

I smile. "And you think you succeeded?"

He looks at me naked, lying in front of him. "I know I did."

He rolls the condom down his hard length and lunges on top of me. As we kiss, our bodies undulate in a rhythm that proves this foreplay is completely unnecessary.

I scratch my nails down his back, and whisper a breathy plea into his ear. "I want you in me."

My boldness with him makes me feel high as he plunges himself into me. A satisfied groan from him is drowned out by my own cries of pleasure. I tangle my legs around him as he thrusts hard and fast. His needy mouth claims all the skin it can reach, kissing my breast, licking my neck, biting my ear. I don't want this ride to end. My hands find their way to his hair and I clutch his locks, tugging his like he did mine before. His gaze flashes up to mine, staring at me with a fiery glare. He watches me intently while he plunges himself into me repeatedly, harder, quicker. My body winds tighter and tighter.

"You feel so good," I say, panting and squirming beneath him.

He responds with another growl, his desire for me bringing out a more animalistic side to him. I love it. I want more. I want to see how far he likes to push things. With him, I feel liberated. I can do anything. And he can do anything...to me.

Miles clutches my ass and lifts me up again, still inside me. He sets me on the arm of the couch where he can reach me standing. I cling to his hips with my legs while gripping the couch to hold myself upright. It's not just the feel of him that's becoming too overwhelming to bear. And it's not just the sight of him as our bodies writhe. It's the mirror on the other side of the room. From here, I have a perfect view of Miles from behind—my legs around him, his body thrusting, his hands running along my body, massaging my breasts and searching for my hands. Our fingers intertwine, and I squeeze his hands, not wanting to let go, ever.

The intensity builds within me, and I feel myself about to come undone. My breath quickens, my eyes close, and I thrust forward, biting into his chest as I come. The orgasm overtakes us both, and I feel him grip me tighter as he releases himself in me. We stay here, gasping for breath, Miles's head buried in my hair, until I find the energy to tilt my head up and kiss him. We collapse onto the couch, naked and heart-to-heart.

"So you liked the song?" he asks in a cocky, breathless voice.

"I loved it." I settle closer to him, my head against his chest, listening to his heart race. "Please don't tell me you go through all that trouble for all the women."

"Just you," is all he says. And it's all I need to hear.

* * *

Miles

I'd felt confident about the song, but I didn't anticipate Abby's reaction. Last night, she proved she's been feeling just as confused about me as I've felt about her. There's something here worth pursuing. All the women I've been with, none of them have made me feel like this.

Sunlight's streaming through the hotel room window. I sit up in bed, rubbing my eyes and glance at the clock on the side table. It's only noon. I look next to me where Abby's gorgeous naked body is barely covered by the sheets. She's in a deep sleep and I don't want to wake her. I kept her busy last night. Three times.

I lean down and kiss her bare shoulder before pulling the sheet up higher, covering her. Then I stumble from the bed and find my clothes. Quietly, I leave the room in search for coffee. Nate's sitting in the love seat by the big windows smoking a joint. I wander over and steal it from him, taking a puff. The hot smoke burns my lungs, and as I exhale my entire body feels lighter.

"How was your night?" Nate asks, amused. I'm certain these walls aren't soundproof, and Abby and I were enjoying each other into the early hours of the morning.

"Fucking fantastic, if I do say so myself."

"I couldn't land that ass, but you did." Nate shakes his head in disappointment. "Unbelievable."

"Nah," I say, taking another hit off the joint and handing it back to him. "I believe it just fine."

I turn toward the kitchen, and Ken comes storming out, stopping two feet in front of me. She's fuming.

"What the hell did you do?"

"What are you talking about?" Don't tell me she's having Devon issues again. I'm feeling better than I have in a long time. I don't need her buzzkill drama.

"You fucked her, didn't you? You're sleeping with the enemy."

I laugh at her. "Thanks for the cliché, but it's none of your business. And she's not the enemy." She's always been jealous about my relationships. Ken's got a tendency to intrude on other people's lives. Which makes me realize... "Are you the reason she wasn't talking to me? Did you say something to her?"

"No." She shrugs, but I bet she's lying. "And if you don't think she's using you, you're delusional."

I shake my head, not interested in this bullshit. I push past her to go find some caffeine, but she stays on my tail, and when we reach the countertop, she stops me.

"See for yourself, Miles."

Kennedy opens Abby's laptop and points to the screen.

"What the fuck are you doing messing with her stuff?"

Before she answers, I notice what she's trying to show me. An email. From a fucking tabloid.

In regard to the topic we discussed, please know the monetary agreement still stands. One story. $50,000.

"What the hell is this, Ken?"

"Ask your new girlfriend."

I drop onto the bar stool, still staring at the screen. What's Abby up to? She was so sincere last night. Full of passion and undeniably into it, but was she just doing it for some fucking money? Am I her research?

"Told you, big bro. Should've stayed away." Kennedy skips into the kitchen and starts prepping coffee for me as if she suddenly gives a shit about my well-being. I don't know what to think about any of this. Is Abby a liar? Is she using me? Is Kennedy actually right for once? Fuck. So much for my great mood.

Ken brings over a steaming mug and sets it in front of me, snapping the laptop closed. "You have no idea what you've gotten yourself into."

The Lust List

The Lust List - Take Your Pick

They're the world's sexiest bachelors. The men of *ScandalLust* mag's infamous Lust List are young, wealthy, and, oh, did we mention? *Hot.*

When scandal follows them everywhere, there's no hiding from the cameras. They're irresistible, insatiable—and talented in all the right ways. Every woman wants them. But these playboys won't be easy to catch...

The Lust List

Miles Riot

by Mira Bailee

HEART STRINGS
BROKEN STRINGS
STRINGS ATTACHED

AVAILABLE NOW

Acknowledgments

To my family, who supports my wildest dreams; my friends, who think I'm awesome no matter what I do; my editor, Nicole Bailey, who makes all my words much prettier; Najla Qamber, who designs the sexiest book covers; Nova Raines, who took on the challenge of co-authoring this massive series with me; and all my readers, who make this adventure worthwhile—

Thank you.

.

About Mira Bailee

Mira Bailee, a beer-brewing librarian, has been writing leisurely, scholarly, and professionally for the past twenty years.

While she's always maintained a high standard of chaos in her daily routine, *The Lust List* allows her to pass on some of her hectic lifestyle to her characters. Her storytelling balances humor and pleasure with sincerity and conflict, providing a wild ride of human emotions.

In the past she studied filmmaking and screenwriting and determined what goes on behind the scenes is just as tantalizing as what's seen in front of the camera. This revelation is the basis for her inspiration for *The Lust List*.